Survival Arts

Ian Wedde was born in Blenheim in 1946 and has an MA with first class honours from Auckland University. He has travelled widely in Asia, the Middle East, Europe and North America and has worked at a wide variety of jobs. He currently lives in Roseneath, Wellington, and earns his living as a freelance writer. He has received a number of prominent literary awards, including National Book Awards for fiction in 1976 and poetry (shared) in 1977. He received the Burns Fellowship in 1972, the Writer's Bursary in 1974, the New Zealand Literary Fund Scholarship in Letters in 1980 and the Victoria University Literary Fellowship in 1984.

Ian Wedde is a major New Zealand poet and has written a number of books of poetry as well as being widely published in anthologies and periodicals. He has written two novels, *Dick Seddon's Great Dive* (1976) and *Symmes Hole* (1986), and a book of short stories, *The Shirt Factory and Other Stories* (1981). He also co-edited with Harvey McQueen *The Penguin Book of New Zealand Verse* (1985).

Ian Wedde

SURVIVAL ARTS

PENGUIN BOOKS

Penguin Books (N.Z.) Ltd, 182–190 Wairau Road, Auckland 10, New Zealand
Penguin Books Ltd, 27 Wrights Lane, London W8 5TZ (Publishing & Editorial)
and Harmondsworth, Middlesex, England (Distribution & Warehouse)
Viking Penguin Inc., 40 West 23rd Street, New York, New York 10010, U.S.A.
Penguin Books Australia Ltd, Ringwood, Victoria, Australia
Penguin Books Canada Limited, 2801 John Street, Markham, Ontario,
Canada L3R 1B4

First published 1988
Copyright © Ian Wedde, 1988
All rights reserved

Typeset in Plantin by Typocrafters Ltd, Auckland
Printed in Hong Kong

First Day 9

Second Day 63

Third Day 123

Afternoon a Day Later 163

. . . we sometimes find a treble superposition of parasites, as in the oil beetles; and we see the maggot itself, the sinister guest at the last feast of all, feed some thirty brigands with its substance.

— Maurice Maeterlinck, Preface to J. H. Fabre's
The Life of the Spider, Hodder and Stoughton, London, 1912

To know how not to know might well be the last word of wisdom.

— J. H. Fabre

Burning thirst of a hundred years constantly waiting,
and today joy arrives as though in a dream.
The sky so calm, unbelievably blue,
the face of the earth peaceful with the sleep of children.

— To Huu, 28 January 1973, Hanoi.
From *Blood and Flowers*,
Foreign Language Publishing House, Hanoi, 1978

First Day

First Day

1

IT WAS LATE IN THE DAY AND STILL SALVATION WASN'T HOME.

'But you can call me Salvo.' Salvation was seldom this pally. Even so, that stupid auction mart manager hadn't stopped to listen.

His leg was hurting like a bastard and the phantom of his sundown fix came to whisper melancholy in his ear. Even the Thais hadn't known where the firing came from back then — heads swivelling wildly on their necks as the stuff sliced the foliage to shreds, and then it stopped. Just someone scared, or protecting their investment.

'*Mring kongvial*,' spirit animal guardian. Salvation's tinny voice rattled the Khmer words. He could have been cursing.

It had been when he tried to stand up again into the silence from which the echoes of firing and the sounds of birds had just departed that he found out about his leg.

Now *that* was an investment he was going to demand some returns on — they were going to be there at the wharf waving flags when he came home from the wars, they were going to be at home to open the door when he got that much further; and when he stepped inside the secure place they were going to pay attention to his needs.

Salvation drove slowly by Wellington harbour. The early summer sunset incinerated the glass towers of the city across the bay. Like everything, it was an illusion. The terrible peace of the place had to be challenged before everyone believed it. Real flames would have to sprout from those innocent mirrors, these children would have to face the ambient threat.

He trod upon the accelerator — the automatic gears, changing suddenly down, lurched the Valiant into blue shadow on the eastern side of the hill — squeal of tyres as Salvation turned the corner from that vision of innocence in flames.

Now the harbour he passed was in shadow, except where the late rays of sun fell upon the air-force base across the water, transforming it into a film-set trading post. Like everything along this route, its innocence reminded him of the past. You wouldn't have called them a 'hospital', those open sheds by the beach at Klaeng, looking west across the Gulf of Thailand. But heroin was the only thing they weren't short of — that, and the little shoal fish flung glittering into baskets from nets which seemed to have trapped the day-long dazzle of the shallows.

Eat fish again, and then the evening shot that became more expensive the longer his leg refused to heal, and watch the sun go down like in a tourist brochure for Thai Air, sinking into the gulf in slow motion through the foreground filigree of palms. The pain would sink, too — he'd even be glad to have eaten the fish. It was the only time of day he could stand to hear the bicycle bells, the racket of the stalls under their kerosene lamps down along the road.

Even the loudspeakers they rigged up by the stereo and cas-sette shack at the corner didn't spoil that hour or two, though later when his dressing got changed he couldn't stand the Thai pop music with its slyly ingratiating woodwind line and the female vocalists whose caterwaulings turned up the truth behind those sloe-eyed myths.

The traffic thickened up by the tavern at Greta Point, and Salvation saw a red Porsche shoot the gap between a car turning into the carpark and another turning out into the traffic. That was not too bad at all — he marvelled, while the bewildered drivers went for their horns and the red car flicked itself out of sight down toward the marina. There was talent around, sure enough, cursed Salvation — but how to get to it? And was that the same car as — at the carwash, by the goddamned auction mart, this morning . . . ?

Now, someone who would buy a, someone who would have a use for a *tank* — the red Porsche had returned Salvation to his angry thought — *that* he would have kept an eye on. And that stupid mart prick wouldn't believe the evidence of his own eyes, an *immaculate* M24 Chaffee tank right there in the photograph;

and the stupid prick wanted to stay with the deep-freezes and washing-machines and the garden tools released by death from years of pottering.

A lead on the buyer by public auction of an M24 Chaffee light tank and he might have discovered a crack in this innocent façade, a way — like the one the red Porsche found there through the dreary determination of after-work drinkers. You go through, and there's caterwauling and a sunset that breaks like fire from the mirrors which now give back images of refugees walking through smoke. Of a painted mouth like a wound, wobbling tongue of blood — the Green Latrine in Vientiane, Crock of Suds in Saigon. And of beach resorts like hospitals where your sundowner comes just after you've had to chew your way through so much bony dazzle of daylight pain — stink of fish guts but it's your leg, and under kerosene lamps along the road they're selling American PX stores, fucking truckloads of it, and nothing fits. Sizes for giants. But these are children, walking out of the smoky flare of the lamps.

Salvation saw the red car turn nimbly into the Evans Bay marina, and he lost it among the lines of trailer-sailers and the tangle of masts that rocked before the blue-shadowed sea.

'Goddamned rich yachties!'

People like that could *afford* a tank.

2

MORNING SMOKO, WEKA YARNS, SURVIVAL ARTS.

'You're not going to believe this, but,' Snow and them sitting in the sun on the footpath outside the auction mart, 'all you need to catch one's a Huntley and Palmer cream cracker.'

Snag's got this baggy singlet on. She tents it above her bony freckled chest. 'I was sunbathing once, up by the river at Otaki Forks? This weka come up and pecked me on the tit.'

'Musta thought it was a raisin,' pipes Ikey.

'Just as well it wasn't you, Ike? Little earthworm there . . .'

'Since when did you ever expose that skeleton to the sun, Snag? Let alone get out of town?'

'Yeah, well? When was the last time you saw past that guts? You need . . .'

'It was in the Sounds,' finish what you start, that's Snow.

'. . . need radar? To get your jandals on?' Snag's laughter almost makes her rattle.

'I wuz getting that sick of fish,' persists Snow. 'Fish for breakfast, fish for . . .'

'Oh yeah?' Ike's getting shrill. 'Well you should be hiring yourself out so kids . . .'

'. . . for dinner, or else it was flaming mussels, I thought . . .'

'. . . study skeletons in school, Snag, look, see, this bit's the . . .'

'Get off, fatguts, leave . . .'

'. . . 's got to be roast *weka*, y'see.' Snow's intonation is dramatic. 'A flaming chicken dinner! All I . . .'

'. . . or what about skeletograms, hey that's a good . . .'

'. . . couldn't get me flaming mind off a juicy roasted . . .'

'. . . some hood wants to deliver a warning, okay,' sopranos Ike. 'You rattle up looking all pale, Snag. "I have a skeletogram here from . . ." . . .'

'Yeah, well, your breath? "I have a breathocontract here from
. . ." . . .'

'. . . dripping fat,' drones Snow. 'Y'see, I'd wake up in the
middle . . .'

'. . . ". . . hhhhhah," victim reels back choking? "No, no, the
breath!" . . .'

'. . . night, got so bad I — *youse listening?*'

'Sorry Snow, this little punk's . . .'

'Okay okay,' Snag's little chest's puffing with rage. 'What was
all that, Snow? The big bush thing? Great white . . .'

'Don't be smart, Snag, give ol' Snow here a . . .'

'. . . great white hunter? — what, Ike? Jus' because you was
getting outclassed there . . . ?'

'Jesus.' Old Snow lights up a Sportsman. 'Don't you flaming
kids ever pipe down?'

Silence. Across the way, the Rub-a-Dub Carwash flails into
action. Sunlight catches in the rear-vision mirrors of grocers'
trucks at the fruit and vegetable market. A thin youth wheels a
deep-freeze from the auction mart to a clapped-out blue J4 van
parked at the bus-stop.

But now: walking stick, a pair of army-surplus camouflage
pants, one leg that swings out in a wide arc, one cheap black shoe
trodden over on its inside edge until the seams have burst — the
rubber foot of the stick jabs down within inches of Snag's skinny
skin-jeans, the busted shoe nearly clips the cigarette from Snow's
upturned face.

They watch the sweat-soaked khaki shirt-back, the long lank
hair and fatigue cap swivel fast into the drive-in doorway of the
auction mart. The man looks over his shoulder, not at them, but
at the street, both directions, and is gone.

'Strike a light,' and the veins in Snow's nose can indeed catch
fire.

'Just another loony,' pipes Ike. 'Tell us about the cream
cracker, Snow.'

'Yeah, well, it's true.' Snow pauses for a yodelling cough. 'All
you need's a cream cracker. It was in the Sounds. I was on me
own. I was getting that sick of fish, fish for breakfast, fish for

dinner, fosh fur . . .'

'Give us a hand?' Two women, one of them stocky, are helping the weedy youth get the freezer into the J4. A trolleybus veers at them with its horn blaring.

'Me?' Ike points at his fat chest. 'Don't suppose you'd want the skeleton there.' They all heave the machine into the van, the skinny fellow ducks in after it.

'Thanks,' barks the stocky woman. She slams the door.

'Oh, don't mention it, my pleasure, always ready to o-blaige,' falsetto Ikey bowing after the departing van. 'What a sourpuss, Christ.'

'Well, you shouldn't have called me "the skeleton",' says Snag. 'Us women stick together.'

'Okay, Snag, next time *you* load the freezer.'

'Didn't even give me a chance, did you? "Who, me? Oh, of course." Well, it just had to be? Didn't it, Mr Muscle?'

Snow's walked off the set. His cigarette butt rolls smoking to the gutter, they hear the high shriek of his cough from inside the mart.

'Bloody ol' Snow better lay off the smokes,' pipes Ikey. He lobs his Coke can into the Council litter bin. 'You want this?' He offers half a pie.

'You must be joking?'

'Please yourself, ungrateful brat.' The pie goes into the bin too.

Across at the Rub-a-Dub, a red Porsche begins luxuriously to emerge. Through the flinging water on the windscreen can be glimpsed the weakly screaming faces of a man and a woman. The woman has bright red hair, an upstanding cockatoo band of it, same colour as the car. In the man's dark face, his mirror sunglasses catch the first light past the Rub-a-Dub's rollers.

'Lookit them?' Snag gawping. 'Some people get all the breaks.'

'Sitting in a *carwash*?' says Ikey. 'Anyway, I thought you was into nature, sunbathing, wekas, all that.'

But she's gone, back to the filing trays and the phone. And Ike too, his eyes hurrying to follow her, steps back inside the auction mart, to where the word '*tank*?' has just been shouted incredulously at the glare of summer light — and then the stick and swivelling khaki leg cutting away fast past a backdrop of greengrocers' trucks revving in a haze of exhaust on the far side of the road — a red trolleybus *this* way . . . a red Porsche *that*.

3

'UGH, GOD, KATE, I COULD NEVER, YOU KNOW, MAKE IT WITH A *meat*-eater!' B.J. steps on the gas.

'You mean like that fat guy back at . . . ?'

'You know, ugh, I'd be all the time thinking about dog's arse-hole, cat's breath, you know?'

'. . . the fat guy back at, with the face like a meat pie, and his . . . ?'

'Give you a hand didn't he?' whines Frank from the back of the J4. 'Hey take it easy B.J. you want me fuckin' crushed or something, should have roped up this . . .'

'. . . did you catch his *breath*, Kate, you know, like an abattoir!'

'Give you a hand didn't he?' In the rear, young Frankie sets his skinny back against the deep-freeze. 'Pull over B.J. Christ's sake you want me squashed here?'

'Yeah, Frank, but did you hear what he said to that poor skinny little punk girl?' Kate's blue eyes, over the seat back.

'Yeah, Frank, you know, called her "the skeleton" didn't he, ha ha, very funny.' B.J.'s dark glasses.

'Jesus B.J. *pull over*!'

B.J. hauls left against the kerb by the new town hall. Its gleaming high-tech glass and stainless-steel walls warp a vista of desultory late-morning traffic, clouds, blue sky and black asphalt. An endless succession of spitting joggers passes the squid-boats at the wharf. Further out, windsurfers are skidding across the harbour. From the attendant's kiosk at the town-hall carpark comes the sound of *DD Smash* singing 'Whaling'.

'Hey, real professional.' Kate's appraising young Frankie's knots. 'You musta been a boy scout.'

'Sea cadet.'

'You wore a sailor's cap, mucked about in whale-boats, all that?'

'Yep, half of us always used to toss up all over the harbour.'

'Hey, neat, B.J., did you know Frankie here was a sailor boy?'

'Run away to sea, eh Frank?' B.J. flags her way back into the traffic.

'To the Labour Department more like it,' jabbers Frankie.

'Whoa, never mind *sailors*,' Kate's launching a drama. 'B.J., did you see that military weirdo at the mart?'

'You back with that Dogbreath character, Kate? The one, you know, that . . . ?'

'Nah, B.J., the paramilitary, the . . .'

'Hey, *I* saw him,' poor young sailor Frank's voice trying to navigate the gap between the two women, 'with the bung leg, with . . .'

'. . . one that was having some kind of shouting match with the guy at the mart, B.J.?'

'*What* guy at the mart, you know, the Dogbreath creep, that . . . ?'

'God, what's the matter with you, B.J., you can't get your mind off that fat joker? I'm talking about . . .'

'Well, it really pissed me off, you know?' Like her driving, B.J.'s voice doesn't have side vision. 'The way he put that little skinny kid down, "the skeleton", *you* heard . . .'

'Yeah, but . . .', comes Frank again.

'But,' Kate wants her drama back, 'I'm not *talking* about him, B.J. I'm talking about the *owner*, "Reliable Reg", that the peculiar guy in military pants . . .'

'. . . but he give you a hand didn't he?' Frank trying the gaps. 'I mean what's so . . . ?'

'Belt up, Frank, me and Kate are having, you know, a discussion here.'

'Yeah, look, sorry Frankie, just shut up a minute will you?'

'I just don't see why you have to put him . . .' Frank sulking to the back corner of the J4. 'Aw, go on then scream at each other, have fun.'

'What makes you think we're fighting, you know, we're just . . .'

19

'Well excuse me B.J. *you know* I'm just confused *you know*, why don't you two lovebirds do it in harmony *you know*, like "Tell me why-y-y-y-y-y-yih, why do we fall in lo-ove?" that you're always fuckin' singing *you know*, shit!'

'Very funny, Frank.' B.J. switches lanes without looking. 'If you can't tell the difference between . . .'

'I mean this ordinary joker, friendly . . .'

'With dogbum breath,' B.J. beginning to yell. '*God*, you weren't even close, Frank, and how do you know that skinny kid . . .'

'. . . *friendly* ordinary joker *you know* B.J. left half his pie on the . . .'

'. . . how do you know, *Frank*, that that "skeleton" wasn't anorexic, huh? Or . . .'

'. . . on the — Anna Rex, what? Who? On the footpath anyway, came and *helped*, and you . . .'

'. . . or that she wasn't in trauma!' B.J. doesn't hear the horns. 'You know. Maybe her father . . .'

'Okay I'll belt up, anything but . . .'

'. . . or her uncle, maybe. You know. I mean these things . . .'

'. . . anything but the fuckin' *lecture* B.J. Christ that's only me in the bottom right-hand corner, you know, all right I'm *out*!', Frank beginning to sing, yell rather, *just can't get used to the sea* . . .

'. . . they *happen*, Frank, you can't just . . .'

'Ah, knock it off, B.J., leave him . . .' Kate's abandoned her drama — her greyed head lolls against the seat back.

'Whew, gee, thanks Kate.' Frank's thin white face by the freezer. 'Maybe you should drive too?'

The J4 jigs its way off the quay into the motorway overpass. Grey cranes give the thumbs-down above deserted wharves. Just offshore, a red motorboat is slowly trolling parallel with the highway. Frankie kneels at the rear window to look back at it. His thin shoulders hump against the receding view. In the driver's seat, B.J. rests her strong forearms on the steering-wheel in a gesture of weariness. Kate reaches across to stroke her back.

Sportsmen with beer cans or motor oil grin out of billboards.

20

B.J. recklessly swoops the van at their smiles and moustaches, their shorts.

'Hey, *sports!*' she hollers.

'What do *they* know,' quiet Kate's hand working at B.J.'s hunched shoulders.

'What's that phrase, you know, "Deep-fry that sucker"?'

'"Deep-fry that sucker!"'

'What's so funny?' surly Frankie turning to where the two women are having all the fun in the front. 'Some ordinary fat guy can't crack a joke but 's okay for youse to have *me* on, that it?'

'Frankie,' murmurs Kate, 'we're not laughing at you, only . . .'

'Only at the *real* men,' yells B.J. 'You know.'

'The *sports,*' Kate. 'Right, B.J.?'

'"Deep-fry that sucker!"'

'Deep-*freeze* that sucker, more like!'

Their merry laughter rattles around the unlined interior of the van. But young Frankie's gazing back at the silence of the blue sea, little red boat upon the deep. He's contemplating yesterday's image of B.J. submerged in the bath-tub beneath a snorkel. What's 'rebirthing'?

4

WALLACE HAD A WAY OF PUTTING HER FOOT DOWN. SHE CALLED
it 'the Istanbul Indicator'. If you start moving before everyone
else, they can see where you're going.

'People just naturally don't want to drive into a Porsche, too,
Jackson.'

'Ooh baby. That bus did. Left, turn *left*. Follow the water. You
the sunrise, Wallace, you the sunset too.'

The blue bay, the hillside of houses — the Porsche ran them
past its drying windows. Ahead rose a hotel like a cereal box. A
crocodile of little children was wending across the promenade,
while their teacher stood in the middle of the road admonishing
the traffic. The Porsche squealed lightly to a halt and the double
file of little faces peered in at the woman with hair like a fire,
the man who looked like a Secret Identity.

'Look at that, Jackson, aren't they sweet, our future?'

'You think them teacher can be trusted with them?'

'*Them* teacher, excuse me, Jackson, goes home and disciplines
her mind with gin, then she has her boyfriend turn up the salsa
music and she just *merengues* along with Celia Cruz while the
slave starts at her feet and works his way up.'

'How can you tell?'

'It's the disguise, Jackson, what you're looking at can't be real.
Now surely.'

'"Get the inside on the outside", that it, Wallace?'

'That's it, Jackson. Whip it out!'

The parade of little protruding tongues and rolling eyeballs
passes. Wallace and Jackson watch the teacher's lips moving in
an apologetic but soundless pattern. Then she too slips out of
frame. The blue expanse of the open harbour rushes at the windscreen. A beacon, joggers, windsurfers, an old man with an old
dog, labouring buttocks on bicycles, a marina and a yacht club.

The Porsche tail-wags down a ramp. Ahead is the glitter of water, idle hulls, gulls rising in languid alarm.

'Ooh wah,' says Jackson. His top lip bears a cargo of water beads. 'Now we get out of the freshly washed car, right?'

'We get out, we walk very calmly to the jetty, we go on board, and then we talk our way back through the whole morning.'

'You're so professional, Wallace, Wallace?'

'Jackson, I think you took one too many.'

'What, uh, you mean, Wal', Wal' . . . ?'

''ludes, Jackson, I'm alluding to 'ludes, God, you're so unobtrusive . . .'

Jackson retches without enthusiasm from the open door of the Porsche. A boat-harbour *habitué* looks on from the bollard where his rod arcs into sunlight. Porsche doors don't slam, they close like a full fridge, they seal in promise, freshness.

'You stupid prick, Jackson, I thought you watched television, don't you know any better yet?'

'It's only nerv', nervous, Wallace, I swear, I'll get the hanging of it.'

'You look like Clint Eastwood in Samoan, and you suffer from *nerves*? And that was "get the *hang*", Jackson. Tell me, what would you rather be doing?'

'Rather be, you know, in the carwash.'

'Jackson, we can't spend *too* much time in the carwash, people would notice.'

'Makes me feel so good.'

'Jackson, there are only about six carwashes in this city, such decadence hasn't caught on yet, people like to do their own at weekends, you know, and grow veges, cut grass, that's one carwash per day bar Sunday — that means we show up at every carwash in the damn city at least once a week, sometimes more if you're . . .'

'But a *Porsche*, Wallace . . .'

'. . . if you're that way inclined. Obviously, Jackson, we're not gardening.'

'. . . Wallace, a *Porsche*, they just naturally think you're going to want to . . .'

'Once a week, sometimes more, Clint Eastwood from Apia sits in the carwash in a red Porsche and *appears* to be . . .'

'*No one can see in!*'

'Okay, Jackson, take it easy, we'll go to the one at Lower Hutt this afternoon, now just don't fall in the sea.'

From his sunny bollard, the lone fisherman catches the flash of Jackson's mirror glasses as his head swivels wildly at the top of the companionway. Then the woman with spraycan-red hair follows him down into the big diesel launch.

It's only about eleven. By the door of the flash red car is a little steaming pool of puke. The big launch rocks slightly at its mooring. From within comes the muffled bass thud of music. The fish aren't biting. And there goes that cop car past again.

'Okay, Wallace.'

'Okay, Jackson, feel better?'

'You see that guy with the rod?'

'*Rod?*'

'*Fishing* rod, Wallace, ha ha, what was that crack about television?'

'He was fishing.'

'Wallace, I don't like it here.'

'You don't like it anywhere but the carwash, Jackson.'

'Can I have some of that?' Jackson's voice changes from panic to ingratiation: no transition.

'This is strictly to bring up the nuance in recall, Jackson, we are not having a party.'

'You want me to start?'

'At the very beginning, my boy.'

Jackson's eyes close. With one finger pressed under his bellowing nose, he allows the edges of his vision to sharpen up. Soon he is running the whole thing past again. At breakfast there were footsteps on the jetty! Bad start. While Wallace was in the bank, he saw a Japanese man photograph the Porsche with him sitting in it. That was bad too. By then the carwash was essential. And then . . .

'Oh God!'

'What have you got, Jackson?'

24

'Wallace, Wallace!'

'Here, some . . .'

'It was at the carwash!'

'Easy does it . . .'

'There was this guy. He come out of the auction mart. I mean, talk about "outside", I mean "inside outside"! You see him?'

' — '

'Had on this kind of, like these, how you say, *gorilla* . . .'

'Oh Jackson, relax, that musta been gorillagrams, baby! Just a . . .'

'No, shut up, he was . . .'

'. . . just a *mask*, Jackson, a rubber . . .'

'No, like a *soldier*, Wallace, a gorilla soldier, you know . . .'

' — '

'. . . you know? And he looked straight at me! I mean . . . he come out of there so fast, boy, this funny leg, he was wearing that brown green pants, you know, a cap.'

'The auction mart?'

'That's it! Opposite the carwash.'

'It's okay, Jackson. You get all kinds of weirdos in those places. People who want to collect stuff. People selling all kinds of junk. Trying to tidy up their pathetic lives. Cranks, you know. Nothing there, Jackson.'

'Well, you know, Wallace, *he* was checking it out.'

'People do, Jackson.'

'Sure. Then what. The teacher?'

'*That's* the one, Jackson. Not now, but soon. That's our connection. All of them. All the guardians of the future. All those "outside inside" behaviour modifiers, Jackson. You know they have all those kids to themselves six hours a day. Six hours a day for twelve years!'

'But you only thinking ahead, Wallace, you don't mean . . . ?'

'That "outside inside" teacher saw nothing but you and me in a Porsche, Jackson, but it was a start. My God. How do you think she felt picking up little, with the brown skid, underpants at the swimming pool all afternoon, get up again tomorrow, same thing?'

'Yes, then what. The fisherman? Lots of them joggers?'

'Nothing, Jackson, just normal. You can relax. At ease, tail-gunner.'

'Thank God.'

'It's over for another morning.'

'Thank God.'

'Thank *me*, Jackson.'

'Thank you, Wallace.'

5

'RELIABLE REG'. LIKE SNAG SAID ONCE, HE COULD SELL A KIWI an airsick bag.

'You're not going to believe this, but . . .'

'"All you need's a cream cracker" . . .' Snag sniggers above invoices.

'What?'

'Sorry boss, nothing, one of ol' Snow's . . .'

'That story about the flaming . . . ?'

'The weka, yeah, but he . . .'

'God, Snag, I've heard that one about a hundred . . .'

'. . . he never finished . . .'

' — '

' — '

'What was I saying?'

'You said, "You're not going to believe this, but . . ."'

'That's right, my God!' Reliable Reg's cheeks collapse upon the urgent intake of smoke. 'Did you see that lunatic with the leg?'

'He bought it, he wore it, he lost the other . . . ?'

'Cut it out, Snag, don't be smart.'

'You mean the bozo with the old army gear on? He nearly kicked old Snow in the mouth!'

'Be one way to shut the old sod up — hey, you're not going to believe this . . .'

' — ' Snag's busy fingers pause with a particular piece of paper.

'. . . listen, Snag — he tried to sell me a tank!'

'He what?'

'That character, with the gammy leg, he tried to get me to flog a second-hand tank for him!'

'Tank?' Snag's reading.

27

'Right. Army tank, you know? Little one, from South-East Asia. War surplus.'

'With guns, like a bulldozer, like that?'

'That's right, Snag. He had a photo.'

'*That* was a nutcase, boss.'

'Too right. Reckoned he got it back here in bits, put it together again, it goes.'

'Guns?' She sets the piece of paper aside.

'Don't be pathetic, Snag. I didn't discuss it. I'm a busy man.'

'Could've been sensational, boss, like your sale gimmick that you're always after — park the tank out the front, red flag on the gun, "You need protection, you need Reliable Reg!"'

'Cut it out.'

'Boy, he certainly looked pissed off when he left?'

'I told him to shove it.'

'You think he had, you reckon he . . . ?'

'*Listen*, Snag, remember that truckload of office furniture last month? That those guys reckoned was from a business shifting to new premises? Had the documents, all straight as far as I could see, and the buggers had driven away with it, filing drawers still full of company stuff, the desks even had someone's spare glasses inside, but they'd gone, those guys? After all these . . .'

'Yeah, but a *tank*, it's not . . .'

'. . . after all these years, Snag, I can still fall in over . . .'

'. . . tank's different from a *desk*, I mean that . . .'

'. . . still get taken over a flaming truckload of bent office furniture, I'm not going to start fucking around with . . .'

'Okay, okay, simmer down, Reg, you'll have a . . .'

'. . . flaming *tank*, for God's sake, Snag, Christ!'

'. . . don't go an' have a heart attack, I was only saying . . .'

' — '

'You all right, boss? Reg?'

'He made me that wild, that fruitcake, flaming mad dingbat hippie or something . . . !'

'Looked a bit like he'd been there, to me, boss?'

'Where, the funny farm? Ha ha.'

28

'The war, in the army, somewhere, you know . . .'

'Him? With hair like that? That leg? come off . . .'

'Maybe that's where he got it?'

'Got what? Listen, Snag, I'm a busy . . .'

'Got the leg, Reg?'

'. . . man — leg?'

'And the tank?'

'Tank?'

'In the war?'

'*What* war. Jesus, Snag, cut it out, get back to . . .'

'You started it.' Snag's fingers pick up the piece of paper again.

'The war, ha ha? Ha . . .'

'The story, just like Snow's weka, don't even . . .'

'Snag, would you please belt up about bloody old Snow's weka, if anyone mentions that bird again I'll go plain berserk, so help . . .'

'What about the tank, then?'

'. . . so help me God — *and* the tank, for Christ's sake! No more tank! No more weka! No more, look, Christ, it's nearly lunch, the whole morning, we haven't even, what say you . . .'

'Boss?' Snag waves the invoice. 'You want me to, um — you want me to, *tidy* this, this . . . ?'

'Direct sale, Snag?'

'Yeah, boss, that freezer, just now, this morning.'

'Oh, the *freezer*! Oh, yeah. Cash, Snag, immediate disposal.'

'How much?'

'A grand.'

'A *grand*? Those, with the . . . ?'

'That's right, Snag. Cash. Beans. Deniros. Moulah.'

'. . . with the old J4?'

'That was them, Snag.'

'They didn't look like cash to me?'

'The *cash* looked like cash, Snag!'

'That skinny young . . . ?'

'Right, with the two dykes.'

Snag's face can aim like the front of an axe. '"Dykes?"'

'Yeah, you know. And cash. "We'll take it now," they said. I told them, I said . . .'

'How would you know they were "dykes"?'

'What? Cut it out, Snag, I didn't go to school just . . .'

'I mean, were they wearing . . . ?'

'. . . just to eat the play-lunch . . .'

'. . . wearing badges, or, you know, a sweatshirt with "I am a . . ." . . . ?'

'*What?*'

'. . . "I am a dyke" on it? I mean . . . ?'

'Ah, come off it, Snag, I didn't . . .'

'"I didn't come down in the last shower," right, boss?'

'Hey! Come on, now . . . !'

'I mean, what're you doing, sticking labels on . . . ?'

' — '

'I mean, so what if they . . . ?'

' — '

'Okay.' Snag's hatchet face watches her hands deal with the invoice.

'These two *women*, all right, Snag? These two women said they'd take the damn freezer. I said, no direct sales under auction licence. They said, what's it worth, we'll pay cash, we need it right now, urgent.'

'You said, a grand?' Her fingers are busy again. Bitten nails, bumpy wrist-bones — smart and fast.

'I said, a grand.'

'You might've got, you know, if you'd got six hundred tomorrow, Reg, you'd have thought all your dreams . . . ?'

'Cash, Snag, in the hand, it sang me a little song and I surrendered, Jesus, it asked for political asylum, Snag, now tell the flaming disc we did it tomorrow!'

'Zap — in she goes. "Not lies, just . . ." . . . ?'

'Just survival arts. You're getting the hang of it, Snag.'

'Sounds disgusting . . . ?' She watches Snow trolley a chest of drawers past — the howl of his cough shakes the office glass. 'Wonder why they needed it so bad?'

'Needed what, Snag?'

'The freezer.'

'Must've had something going off at home.' Reliable Reg's dialling.

'Maybe they chop up men?'

'Very funny, Snag.'

'You know, maybe they . . . ?'

'Don't say it, Snag — why doesn't anyone ever answer?'

'"You're not going to believe this, but . . ."'

'That's enough.'

'*And* a tank, boss?'

'And a tank.' He hangs up. 'You know, Snag, you should try running this damn place one day.'

'So should you?' Snag addresses her hands.

'What?'

'Nothing, Reg. Hey — you know what they found in one of the drawers? Of those hot desks?'

'*What*, Snag?'

'"You're not going to . . . ?"'

' — '

'A suicide note, boss.'

'Ha ha.'

'Undated.'

'Very funny.'

'Think so?'

'No.'

'Lunch?'

6

SOME DAYS WHEN FRANK THOUGHT BACK IT WAS ALL HE COULD do to remember what came after.

There he was, a kid, learning knots by Evans Bay. Sometimes they'd pile into the whaler with the gaff-rig and fart about on the harbour. Some of them used to go green and toss up.

And that 'lieutenant', what a shit. 'All right lads now make sure if you absolutely *have* to be sick don't do it into the *wind*.' *Lads*.

Then Uncle Geek would pick him up and they'd get a hamburger in Kilbirnie on the way home. Next thing he knew it was the Labour Department.

What happened in the middle?

'What's up, Frank?'

'I oughta see Uncle Geek.'

'*Who*?' Kate drops her magazine. Her voice arrives unobstructed where Frank crouches by the freezer.

'Uncle Geek. Used to look after me.'

'Didn't do much of a job, Frankie.'

'Come on Kate I mean . . .'

'Well, did he?'

'He was okay.'

'When was the last time you saw him?'

'Just before I run away.'

'Jesus.' Kate ponders. 'And he never tried to find you, Frank?'

'I mean Uncle Geek just didn't have the time.'

'So what did he do with you?'

'Bit of a dag really. Used to get me into all these things. I was, I was a sea cadet like I told you earlier on. There was scouts swimming YMCA soccer outward bound computers, there was all these holiday things, carpentry electrics tramping trips, an' once he sent me to stay with that Barry Crump joker . . .'

'*Geek*, right?'

'. . . and then I run away.'

'And then?'

'I was jus' trying to remember, Kate.'

'Like, *four years*, Frank? And this Geek never even . . . ?'

'Well look at you Kate, I mean what are ya! — teacher, lawyer, a fuckin' doctor or something?'

'I had a kid, Jane, she lives with her father in Aussie.'

'*You* . . . ?'

'That's what *I* was.'

'You? A kid?' Frank puts down his screwdriver.

'Don't say it, Frank.'

'Okay what do I care?' But he's staring across at Kate.

'I even married the bloke.'

'All right.'

'He was so nice I went right off my rocker, Frank.'

'And then . . .'

'Not "And then", Frank. I kicked around a bit before . . .'

'Before B.J.'

'Yeah, Frank — B.J.'

'It's like there's B.C., A.D., and B.J. — a.m., p.m., and fuckin' B.J.!'

'Is there life after B.J., Frank?'

If it was a joke, they'd both be laughing. Frank resumes with the screwdriver, 'What's this "rebirthing", Kate — B.J. in the bath with a snorkel?'

'Something she's trying out.'

'What about standing in the back yard yelling "I want to live, live, live!"? What's all that about?'

'Affirmation.'

'Hey, Kate — what's about this freezer here? I mean, it's . . .'

'Never you worry, Frank me boy, just wire her up.'

'Mr Fixit.'

'That's you, Frankie.'

'But I mean, straight, why . . . ?'

'Fix anything, make anything, mix anything, break into anything . . .'

'Cut it out, Kate!'

'Sorry, only kidding.'

'This some smart scheme of B.J.'s, Kate?'

Kate's back into her magazine — flicking pages.

'Some brainwave, some scheme, make a . . . ?'

She finds something to settle down and read.

'Listen, it's only fair! Here I am doin' all the dirty work, how do I know you're not up to . . . ?'

'What exactly do you think we could "get up to" with a *freezer*, Frank?'

'You could store drugs.'

'So we could.'

'Is that it?'

'No.' Back to the magazine: serious inclination of the grey head.

And that was Uncle Geek too. Silence would come down so thick you could hear his heart beat. Like a fuckin' clock — yeah, what about the time the house was full of clocks? Taiwanese alarm clocks? And when Uncle Geek was out he'd crawled round the whole lot, wound them all up, set all the alarms for two in the morning, they all went off at once? And Geek screaming? About two hundred? Cl', clocks?

'What's so funny, Frank?'

'Just remembering one time all these clocks — never mind.'

'You only laugh about once a month, Frank.'

'Only get one joke a month.'

'Your monthly, Frank.'

'Ha ha.'

'Sorry.'

'Jus' because you're bent you think . . .'

'I don't think *anything*, Frank, get it? I don't *care*!' She waves the magazine. 'Oh, balls.'

'Kate,' Frank's turn to try a joke, 'how can you *say* that!'

'There's you laughing again, Frankie!'

'Twice in the month!'

'Balls, balls, balls!'

'Knock it, Kate, knock it . . .'

'Deep, deep-freeze, deep . . .'

'. . . knock it off — *what*? Deep, what?'

'Deep-fry. Those suckers.'

'You said, "freeze". You've stopped fuckin' laughing Kate.'

'I meant "fry", Frank.'

'And this morning, too, Kate . . . you an' B.J. cackling away in the van, I heard you, "Deep-freeze . . ." . . .'

But Kate's suddenly looking past him, through the dusty window.

'I *heard* you!'

'*Frank*! Frank, look! — *listen*, remember when we were . . .'

'Change the subject won't you, why . . . ?'

'. . . *listen*, we were at that auction place, across the . . .'

'. . . what's all this mystery, this "deep-freeze" bullshit, what're . . . ?'

'. . . across the — listen, shut up?' She's on her feet. 'Across at the carwash there was this flash red car with two people in it? Whacked, or something, they were in the Rub-a-Dub about the time we . . . ?'

'. . . what're you and B.J. up to, *Kate*?'

'. . . they were sitting in the car? Well, they . . .'

'*What's going on?*'

'They just drove past, Frank!' Is this Kate's passion for drama? 'Is what's going on!'

'Who did?'

'The people in that red . . . remember?' She mimes the fast car.

'The Porsche?'

'That red car this morning. It just cruised . . .'

'Come off it, you wouldn't even know the kind of, the make of . . .'

'I know the woman's hair, like a flaming cockatoo on fire . . .'

'Hey, that's . . .'

'Right?' And she's off. 'How'd they know we lived in Lower Hutt?'

'*Right*, that's right, she — why would they want to?'

But Kate's long leg's through the door. 'Maybe they don't.'

That greyed head whizzes past the front window, and when he catches up she's backing the van into the street.

'Wait for me!'

'Stay here. B.J.'s on her way.'

'Where . . . ?'

'. . . let's see what Lower Hutt's got, that they . . .', find the gear, *any* gear, '. . . need so badly,' and off.

At the corner, a whisk of red turning right across a light-industrial vista, little frame of a factory carpark with a giant paint pot — and the J4 turning too. Frank watches it go, trailing smoke.

Why did it matter?

And that's just like old Geek, too — Frank mopes back inside to the freezer — watching him go, tearing off. Like the time he bought up all them Railways uniforms, tore up to Auckland overnight and sold them back to the Railways there for a massive
. . .

'*Third* time this month!' Frank's laughing all by himself.

Something's happening.

7

FIRST THE DELUGE, SHIFTING THE BORED FACE OF THE FAT MAN in the cashier's booth into another warping plane. The water pours thickly down over the windows, you could almost be under the surface, breathing . . .

'*Après nous le déluge!*'

'Ah . . . ah . . .', Jackson's face has an invisible aqualung in it, his mouth gone frog-like around a phantom tube of air. The whole car begins to vibrate as the rollers spin into motion against its sides. Then a huge clump of writhing tentacles like green egg-noodles descends upon the roof, and Jackson's aqualung starts to pump him.

'Now, Jackson?'

'*Naow*, Wallace!'

See the monsters of the deep . . . kiss me.

Great felt drums begin to softly batter the Porsche. With a departing slither, the green tentacles slide down the rear window. A sudden sunlit jet of fresh water smites the wind-screen. Something wrenches the aqualung from Jackson's mouth, for a moment he's breathing water. Then they break surface into the real world where two youths assault the dripping flanks of the car with drying rags.

Jackson looks around himself in the first bliss of rebirth.

'Christ, Jackson, put it away will you?'

The car grumbles forward into a seedy light-industrial side-street. A giant paint pot hangs suspended above a corrugated-iron façade.

'Thank you, Wallace.'

But Wallace's silence suggests that carwash twice a day is out of reach of gratitude. Getting 'the inside on the outside' has not paid off with Jackson. See? — only minutes out of the carwash, and already he's going to pieces again. Grabbing at her, a grotesque expression of fear mocking the Third World Eastwood face.

'Listen, Jackson, I think . . .'

' — '

'. . . I really think it's time we . . .'

'Wa' . . .'

'*What*?' But now Wallace has seen it too — the battered blue J4 van that has blatantly pulled in behind the Porsche. In the rear-vision mirror, her eyes cull Kate's face from the dusty refractions of the van's windscreen. You don't need to watch too much television to spot this for a tail.

'That, they, this, at . . .'

'Right, Jackson, they were at the mart this morning when we . . .'

'It wasn't the . . .'

'Right, Jackson, it *wasn't* the military dude . . . *how did you miss them, Jackson*? What's the matter with you?'

'It's the first time, Wallace. I never lost anything before!'

'Too much goddamn carwash, Jackson, you're going soft, heh heh . . .', Wallace dropping the gearshift back, accelerating past a queue of cars moving ahead on a green light. An early left, around the block, and sure enough there's the J4 ahead, taking a lumbering bewildered left corner itself.

'See, they after us, Wallace!'

'Couple of women in a disgusting old . . .'

'There was a man.'

'Call that a man?'

Entering the silence of its own speed, red laser streak along the foreshore, tunnelling through sunlight, the Porsche leaves behind the confident billboards, man on a ladder slapping up a four-foot high can of motor oil in an athlete's hand, or maybe it's beer. No sign of a J4 in the rear-vision mirror, not very likely. Like a rear turret gunner, Jackson stares aft.

'Never before, Wallace . . . what's wrong with me?'

'It's time to move.'

'Where?' whimpers Jackson. 'Wherever you are, I mean . . .'

'Make a move . . .'

'I mean, wherever you . . .'

'Stop whining, Jackson. I mean, it's time . . .'

'. . . make our move. That's . . .'

'. . . wherever you are, there's . . .'

'. . . there's nowhere to go, Wallace. What?'

'. . . that's all.'

'What's . . . ?'

'Good grief, Jackson, you've really lost the place — can't you see where . . . ?'

'Where are we going?'

'Nowhere. Forget it.'

But as he stares back, it seems to Jackson that the whole world is reeling itself in under the Porsche. There's always new stuff just where you are. And, if you look forward, where Wallace's head of flames inclines angrily at the possible, it's all coming at you so fast you . . .

Somewhere's in front and behind as well. Where's Nowhere? And he's never forgotten anything before.

'What's happening, Wallace?'

'It's time to make our move. Enough farting around in car-washes. It could've gone on forever. Who knows, you might have gone up to three, even four carwashes a day, I mean . . .'

'I do my work!'

'You lost it just when . . .'

Quite suddenly, Jackson utters therapeutically primal roars. He shakes his head and flails fists at the ceiling of the Porsche. His dark glasses fall off.

'What?'

'That was . . .'

'Jackson, I think you're improving!'

'Wallace.'

'Spiderman.'

'What?'

'I said, "*Spiderman*".'

Across the harbour, shafts of sun pierce the clouds, falling like innocent stage lights upon the mock-up of a toy city.

'Can we get ice-cream cake, Wallace?'

8

WHAT THE HELL COULD YOU HAVE SAID FOR THE PLACE?

Salvation's double-tracking — he's driving his Valiant down the trail between innocence and vengeance.

Birthplace of the poet Santhorn Bhu (1786–1855), on the Sukhumvit Road from Bangkok. *Pom yoo thi nai*: where am I? Klaeng, 250 kilometres down the Sukhumvit Road from the Camillan Hospital, also on the Sukhumvit Road. Also on the Sukhumvit Road was the British Dispensary.

Then the road went for 250 kilometres with mountains and forest on the left and the Gulf of Thailand somewhere on the right, with mangroves in the river-mouths and plenty of crocodiles, and out at sea gigantic sharks. When they fished sharks up at Klaeng he'd sometimes got a piece instead of the bony sprats, but neither without chilli. *Ah harn chao, ah harn klang wan, ah harn kam*: breakfast, lunch, dinner.

Then the good old Sukhumvit Road went on through Chanthaburi. Left, the Cardamom Mountains, and forest no one knows ways through, except those who don't tell, monkey-meat men. 400 km on from the British Dispensary in Bangkok and you find Trad. Little road to Laem Sok on the Gulf. Offshore, Koh Chang Island. A track, no more, to the Kampuchean border. He still wants to call it Cambodia, or the Khmer Republic even. A very long way inland to Phnom Penh. About a lifetime north to Laos, up the Mekong. Vientiane.

Of course, *he* did it the other way round. *Pom yoo thi nai?* Cardamom Mountains on the *right*. Sharks and crocodiles on the *left*. British Dispensary 400 km *ahead*, also Camillan Hospital. Along the way: Klaeng, poems of Bhu, sun down into Gulf of Thailand, fish supper, *ah harn kam*, maybe shark.

Then — '*Dai prod*?' (Please) . . . '*Khob khun* . . .' (Thank you). His sundowner. The bicycle bells that then faded pleasingly back

40

as the velvet dark rose between the kerosene lamps. Nodding to
sleep to the caterwauling lullabies from the stereo shack. This
was an unspoiled fishing village. Somewhere in the back of the
noise he could always detect traces of Bhumibol Adulyadej's
clarinet.

All he had to read was Panineau's guide to Bangkok, 'City of
Enchantment'. It didn't tell you the difference between *chedi*,
prang, and *prasad*. It mentioned Patpong Road bars, but not
what to do after the midnight curfew. It told you the New
Zealand Embassy was in Silom Road. He didn't doubt the
information, didn't go there either.

In Vietnam they'd had this thing: you don't go calling people
by name, you have to outwit the spirits.

Who calls for whom?

Who is who?

Who calls and to whom does someone answer?

Who answers?

He who calls for his wife.

So, you see, you'd get the information in the end, same as
you'd get the CBU bombs out of the F-105.

Now he's skirted the head of the harbour. Back across, the way
he's come, he can see the Evans Bay marina where the Porsche
vanished — real Saigon taxi style, that. His evening ritual — to
drive around the Miramar Peninsula through the Shelly Bay
Base, through Scorching Bay, across to Breaker Bay, all the way
round to where Island Bay looks back across at some final pink
far-off gleam of light on the snow-peaks of the Seaward Kai-
kouras — it's a shape of motion like the one that had led him
back, back then, through Klaeng's beachfront rehabilitation and
the healing serenades of Bhumibol Adulyadej's Thai-jazz clarinet, to the end of the Sukhumvit Road.

Other thing, in Viet Nam, these kids' poems:

> A grey trunk comes first
> Then come two thick forelegs
> Then come two thick hindlegs
> A tail comes last

41

And what's *that* (outwitting the spirits)?

> A tail comes first
> Then two thick hindlegs
> Then two thick forelegs
> Where is the trunk keeping itself?

They turned it round, see? That's how they sang it after the Revolution. The great elephant had fallen apart.

Salvation steps on the Valiant's gas.

The view down to the open Pacific does not make him think of the Gulf of Thailand; but the vestige of sunset and the pain in his leg return a fish taste to his mouth, and sweat, like chilli sweat, soaks the back of his khaki shirt.

'*Dai prod?*' (Please . . .), but no 'Thank you' (*Khob khun*), not in Island Bay, nor in a town where not a single merchant adventurer will look an M24 in the eye and say *Chan tong garn man*: 'I want it!'

Who calls and to whom does someone answer? And what exactly did that sad honest sack expect the evil spirits to call down, Shrike missiles? Into Wakefield Street, Wellington? Clapped-out lawnmowers, retired rakes, and deep-freezes, more likely, and even that was enough to give the creep a heart attack.

'Call me Salvo!' Salvation's choking with a kind of laughter, same as when he'd asked to be taken to the Somerset Maugham suite, Oriental Hotel, they pay attention to your needs there; but he'd got Klaeng, fish, and a sundowner that took away his *bhat* as well as his will to study the first of the Buddha's Four Noble Truths, namely, Life is subject to suffering.

Ahead are the lights of Island Bay, another unspoiled fishing village, where at last his M24 Chaffee awaits him in its shed, in his secure place. For a moment his thoughts return to the red Porsche and his feeling that there are untapped resources. It's like he needs to chuck away the guide-book. Throw away the script. It doesn't say what happens off Patpong Road between one in the morning and dawn, like it doesn't tell you who in this city of second-hand deep-freezes wants to buy a tank.

9

MEMORY CROSSES JACKSON'S FACE AS A TSUNAMI DOES AN ATOLL.
'Are you ready for what I'm going to tell you, Wallace?'
'What's that, Spiderman?'
And ebbs just as fast. 'Why *Spiderman*, Wallace?'
'Since you seem to be about ready, post-carwash, or should I
say *après*-carwash, in your afterglow, Jackson, and capable of
anger, I'll tell you. You want some of this, it really ties up the
loose ends?'
'Thank you, Wallace.'
'I *like* the way you say that.'
'Say what?'
'Thank you.'
'What for?'
' — '
'Wait, Wallace — *I* was going to tell, you were going to have
to be . . .'
'But Jackson, you know nothing . . .'
'. . . be ready, Wallace.'
'. . . know nothing about spiders — what? Ready for what?'
'It got nothing to do with them spider!'
'Jackson, that's what I . . .'
'I was going to . . .'
'. . . I was going to tell you about.'
'That what *I* was going to say!' Jackson's shrieks batter back
and forth in the cabin. The colour of peeled bananas, Wallace's
thighs step to block his vision of his own television-screen-sized
face reflected in a little porthole. Where the bananas join up, her
bright red . . .
'For God's sake, Jackson, don't go haywire.'
'Wallace, I . . .'
'Calm down, now take that off too.'

43

'Wallace, I just trying to . . .'

'And meanwhile I'll . . .'

'. . . to tell you about . . .'

'. . . tell you about — *what*?'

'You doing it again!'

'Jackson, stop!'

'But I not started yet!'

'Not *that*.'

'Not what, Wallace? Not stop what . . . ?'

'I said don't stop *that*, Jackson, just . . .'

'Okay, you ready?'

'. . . just listen — what? Ready for . . . ?'

'*Wallace! The cake!*'

Ice-cream gateau squeezes through between the banana thighs where the full pale weight of Wallace's bunch has sat upon the mahogany chart table. Myopic even, Jackson scans the way to supper.

'Lick it *all* off. My *God* that's cold, Jackson. All the way round, fella.'

Too mouth-full to speak, Jackson's dark, cream-smeared face scarcely looks up from its charting as Wallace tries once again to educate him about the red-streaked spiders. *Latrodectus katipo*. What *else* have we got, Jackson, she's saying, when his attention to the fiery glacial maps of her body suddenly wavers.

'. . . I mean, nothing, right, Jackson? That's the only — hey, don't *stop*!'

'Wallace, I just forgot . . .'

'There's not much to . . .'

'. . . to tell, you ready? — to tell you . . .'

'. . . not that much to remember, I'm ready, just . . .'

'. . . tell you about . . .'

'. . . just shut up, find the place, just remember that, tell me later!'

'I just remembered . . .'

'Good boy, Jackson, don't forget. Shut up. Oh my God.'

'No, I mean . . .'

'Now! Later! Shut up! Jackson!'

44

'—'
'—'
'Wallace, think I just washed your car, ha ha.'
'Oh Jackson, you anteater, I like that, Jackson. My red car!'
'Ha ha, your red car, Wallace.'
'Now then, Jackson, have you remembered?'
'Yes! Yes! Gorilla!'
'. . . about the red streaks — *gorilla*?'
'Streaks?'
'On the spiders' backs?'
'No, I remember — I forgot . . . !'
'That's why I . . .'
'Wallace, I forgot to tell you, now I remember . . .'
'. . . why I, my hair, the car, in honour of, this red — what?
Whoa, *Jack* . . .', as Jackson's big brown hands clamp her jaw
shut by grabbing her whole head and just *stopping* it, that red-
red-red, that crazy . . .
'Now you listen, Wallace, I saw that man.'
'—'
'That gorilla.'
'—'
'He was just behind us in a car when we got back tonight. The
gorilla. Were you ready, were you ready to hear that? Wallace?
I didn't miss it, see? I remembered!'
'*Gorilla?*' She gets it out through clamped teeth. 'Let me go!'
'Yeah. From the mart, by the carwash, this morning, you said
he was all right.'
'I don't remember. Let me *go*, Jackson!'
'The green pants and the cap with the funny leg . . .'
'Re-*lease* me.'
'Sorry, Wallace. Don't . . .'
'What do you think I am, Jackson, a fucking basketball?'
'. . . don't you remember? Wallace? With the leg?'
But, liberated, Wallace's shouts now occupy all the space in
the below-decks of the launch, whose lights also spill out across
the water, dark now — it's been a long day, and Wallace does *not*
remember a gorilla's leg at the carwash, it was only the first of

two carwashes today, Jackson; any more than you, Jackson, remember the littlest bit about *Latrodectus katipo* with her streak of fire, our saviour; and the shower in this tub couldn't wash cake off a, let alone . . .

But didn't I clean it up, wonders Jackson? Didn't I see that funny leg gorilla fellow this morning, look right at me, and again tonight, behind us? Following us? And them women in the old blue van, this morning and this afternoon, the same? Following? I didn't miss them! They after us?

'What's a *ki te po*?' — this aloud to the door behind which the spiderwoman's handpumping tepid water on her fires.

Now even the carwash isn't safe any more.

10

'I DON'T GET IT,' FRANKIE, BACKLIT BY TELEVISION, STARING AT the summer of 1957, August, in Hiroshima. 'What's going on?'

'They *lost* me, B.J., it's . . .'

B.J. has no time for drama. '*Lost*, Kate?'

'. . . true — what? Yeah, lost.'

'If you guys,' whines Frank, 'don't want to watch this movie, why don't . . .'

And no time for Frank. 'Stop calling us guys, you know, Frank.'

'Shit, B.J., the movie's hard enough . . .'

'B.J., listen! It was . . .'

'. . . hard enough without,' flickering Frank, 'I mean I don't . . .'

B.J. has her topic. 'Start lining up coincidence with, you know, Kate, with . . .'

'. . . don't fuckin' get it anyway, why don't . . .'

'. . . coincidence with purpose, Kate, you know, you end up with the same old passive . . .'

'It was *deliberate*, B.J.! They *lost* me!'

'Why don't you guys,' peering at subtitles, 'go and have your fight . . .'

'*Guys*?'

'B.J., listen, those, that red . . .' Kate's grabbing B.J.'s humped-up shoulders.

'Hang on, Kate — Frank, you know, if you say that one more . . .'

'I know, I know, "Shut up", just switch me on when you . . .'

'. . . B.J., they *deliberately* shook me off! The red car people! They lost me!'

B.J.'s shoulders are up by her ears now. 'Maybe you watch too much television. You know, Kate, this confusion of . . .'

'. . . when you need the fuckin' freezer rewired or something!'

'. . . of coincidence with purpose, you know, puts you back in the same old passive victim role, Kate, you know, you have to see . . .'

'I don't get you guys — whoops! Sorry! *Four* laughs, four . . .'

'Christ, don't you talk down to me, B.J.! I'm . . .'

'. . . four times,' sniggers Frank, 'this month!'

'*Now* what're you laughing about, Frank?'

'Nothing, B.J., just a joke me and . . .'

'B.J., I'm not a . . .'

'. . . me and Katie . . .'

'. . . not a schoolgirl, B.J. — God!'

But now it's Frank who's got B.J.'s shoulders squared at him. 'Did you say "me and Katie", Frank? You know, "you and Katie"?'

'Yeah, what's . . .'

'What's this, Kate — you know, you and Frank having . . .'

'Here we fuckin' go . . .'

'. . . having little jokes? You and Frank? Kate?'

'. . . here we go again,' and Frank swings his lost attention back to black-and-white A-bomb victims — a conversation about the impossibility of talking about Hiroshima . . . a French woman in her thirties . . . a Japanese man.

'What on earth are you on about, B.J.?' Kate's dove voice.

'You know, you and . . .'

'Listen — this afternoon, B.J., me and Frank . . .'

'"Me and Frank" . . . ! Kate, you know, I thought I told you . . .'

'B.J., what're you *talking* . . .'

'I *told* you, Kate — you know, we can't go getting all confidential with . . .'

'God, B.J. — what're you talking about, you stupid bitch!'

On the screen, a size you can see if you move really close to get away from all the aggravation, the argument — B.J. and Katie going for each other like he wasn't hardly even there — on the screen there's been these naked shoulders, different skin colours, and this man saying in French (the subtitles come on

48

down toward where the bum started) *You haven't seen anything in Hiroshima*. He kept saying it. The woman kept saying what she'd seen in the hospital, in the museum. You saw bits and pieces of it happening, burnt people, smoke, a woman running out of the smoke. The man who was talking had very smooth Japanese skin. Then the woman was watching him sleep. His hands were twitching. Then they had a shower. No way you could keep up with what they were saying. You had to read it clicking across in the subtitles. Then he kept saying *I'd like to see you again*. Then they were outside in a noisy street, but normal — no kids walking out of smoke with their skin hanging off. He was wearing a business suit.

That was about where Frank lost track again, because all at once he saw the woman asleep in the middle of some kind of demonstration, and the man with the smooth shoulders stopping and looking at her. Then, when she woke, they had this talk. You could see they really wanted to fuck. These kids, this demonstration, kept on, with placards about peace. Then the woman and the man disappeared into the crowd. Now, here they are, in a house. And you keep getting these shots of somewhere else, not Japan. Rivers, jetties, poplars. And here the woman is, with the Japanese man, in the house. She's shouting *I want to get out of here*! She's hanging on to the man. It's dark.

What's all this about?

And when he looks round to say, couldn't one of you guys, whoops, one of youse tell me what's going on in this movie, he sees B.J. and Kate hanging on to each other too, and looking at *him*, not at the movie. Both staring at him, not saying a thing.

'Frank, you tell B.J. what happened this arvo.' Kate's rubbing away at B.J.'s shoulders.

'You mean with the deep-freeze?'

'No, no Frankie. The red car. And that was "fry".'

'You said "deep-freeze" Kate, don't bullshit me, and this morning too, youse guys . . .'

'*Frank*.'

'B.J.,' Frank's face trembling in television light, 'I'm only trying . . .'

'Frank, that's from Garfield cat comics, that funny fat cat's always saying "Deep-fry that sucker!", it's . . .'

'. . . trying to tell you what — B.J., I'm only trying to tell you . . .'

'. . . it's only a kind of silly joke with me and B.J., Frank!' Kate's soothing voice. 'That "freeze", that was just . . .'

'. . . tell you what happened this afternoon,' whines backlit shaky Frank, 'I'm trying — but that "freezer" and "balls" — B.J., that's *twice* I've . . . !'

B.J. humps forward. 'You know, just forget the freezer!'

'Well okay, B.J., but *you know*,' Frank displays the words between them, '*you know*, why . . .?'

'Forget it, Frank! Tell me . . .'

'That's right, Frank — tell B.J. about the red . . .'

'Why'd ya fuckin' get it then? The freezer?'

On screen, behind Frank, they sit in a restaurant or café. Below them a river flows. The place is almost deserted. They're sitting with their heads almost together.

B.J. and Kate looking at each other. Television voices speaking in French. Kate's slowly shaking her head.

'Frozen meat. Survival rations.' But she's still looking at B.J. — a smile twitches her lips.

'But you don't,' whimpers Frank, 'fuckin' eat meat.'

'All right, Frank, tell B.J. about the balls joke, then all about the red car.'

'I wasn't even *there* Kate, you just . . .'

'Come on, Frankie. Tell her.'

'B.J., Kate just took off, left me . . .'

'Frankie, it's okay. Just tell her.'

'Kate and me, we had this joke. About having a joke a month. A *monthly*, see? Then there was the bit about the freezer. B.J., I *heard* . . . !'

B.J.'s head comes out of her shoulders like a turtle's from its shell. 'And then?'

'Ah, forget it!' Frank turns back to the mystery of television.

'But then? Tell her, Frank.'

'That red Porsche shot past the window. Kate seen it, I never.

But I seen it go round the corner down the street round by the carwash. Kate took off after it, don't ask me why.' He's staring at the television movie — its shadows flutter across his face. 'I don't . . .'

'See?' Kate's in close with B.J. 'And then I waited — it came out of the carwash, same woman with red hair, a dark joker, they saw me follow them, they shook me off just like in the . . .'

'. . . don't fuckin' get it!' jabbers Frankie.

B.J. neither. 'I don't get it. You know, why should they care?'

'But B.J. — two carwashes a day? One of them where we're buying the, the whatsit, the other round the corner from where we . . .'

'I fuckin' don't get *any* of it,' Frank — we're back with some other place: docks, a different river, back to the Japanese man with his head in his hands, back to the other place. '. . . don't get youse, don't get . . .'

'B.J., from your vast store of wisdom, tell me, how many red Porsches with weird people in are going to be . . .'

'. . . don't get the fuckin' freezer, don't get this movie, don't . . .'

'. . . just when we, or where we . . . ?'

'Stop *whining*, Frank! Well, you know, Kate, why the hell should they . . .?'

'I don't *know*, B.J.! But they did!'

B.J.'s 'leadership qualities'. 'Take it from the other end, you know, Kate? How could they know?'

'Know *what*?' Quick as a flash, Frank. Frank had learned to seize hints. He got that much from Geek. As the holidays had approached, he'd got used to reading the signals in Uncle Geek's words. What was it to be this time? Canoeing, with ice-water and rocks? Ropes down mountains? Hours rewiring old radios? Flow-charts, a computer instructor who felt him up and made dumb jokes about his apples? One hint, key word, 'You keen on,' get set, '*bush*?', and Geek's grin, that was it, go, run, fuck off! 'Know *what*, you guys? I heard that, B.J. I'm not stupid *you know*. What's "*what*"? and a th', a fuckin' *grand*? For it? For a clapped-out freezer?'

51

A young woman seems to be licking blood off herself, in that other place. Her hair cropped short. When she runs, the flicker of her movement crosses Frank's hunting features.

B.J. doesn't even hear the 'guys'. She reaches over and switches off World Cinema. Kate has this little sad smile on her face.

Come to think of it, she looks a bit like that woman in — not in Hiroshima, the one in the other place, with the cropped . . .

B.J.'s shoulders drop, she spreads her arms in a gesture that could be surrender or welcome — her voice hesitates between the two. 'Frank, Kate, I think we are going to have to make, you know, a decision.'

Key word. Alone, it enters Frank's mind: *we*.

First time he's ever been going to be in a *we*.

11

PUBS ARE SHUT, TV'S OVER – THE WARM EARLY SUMMER WIND
shifts fast-food wrappings in the downtown malls. The kids are
gone, the ghetto-blasters. By the Bank of New Zealand steps near
the fountain, a plastic snort-bag floats in the pond like a
diaphanous iceberg. Tawdry moontrails of streetlights in the
water. And here comes the flashlight of a policeman, flicking
over the plateglass, into the inset shadows of entranceways.
Ambient phantoms of music, distant carousing shouts and
smashing of glass, desultory roar of traffic on the arterial
throughways. Overhead, the stars slip in and out of sultry cloud-
cover, tawny with the city's footlights.

In a City Council Parks Department enclave of flax bushes,
discover old Snow. Too bloody steep, the steps, and too many,
to where his lock awaits the erratic gougings of its key.

And too dark the night, too treacherous the surface of the
earth, for Ikey there to venture forth before digesting the Green
Parrot's steak-and-eggs.

The city air precipitates its dust upon them, and the wind
claps flax leaves together by their heads.

From the flax bush, above the dead-of-night mutter and rave
of the city, hear the shrill whinny of old Snow's cough.

'Christ, Snow!'

'What's up, son?'

'You better lay off the smokes, smokes, before . . .'

'Before they, flaming, kill me?' Lungs' high howl. 'I'll prob'ly
die, before . . .'

'You, you're not so . . .'

'. . . before the, flaming, smokes, can . . .'

'. . . so antique as all . . .'

'. . . can skittle me, eh!' Hey, hah, *heurp*!

'. . . as all that — *Christ* Snow, sounds like . . .'

53

'What,' hey, hah! '. . . about . . . ?'

'. . . like a *bearing's* gone phut!'

'. . . what about, that flaming, guts of yours, Ike?'

'My friend.'

'Still flaming well, have to carry, it. Need a, flaming, trolley, soon,' trying to get air where only an abrasive fume whistles through the diminishing valve. 'I'll, I'll . . .'

'Fair go, Snow, you need . . .'

'. . . *survive* you!'

'. . . need a spell, somewhere with, with fresh air and stuff!'

'Hospital?'

' — '

'You'd, visit? You, an', and young *Snag* — why'd's she . . . ?'

'Come off it, Snow, I . . .'

'. . . flaming call herself that, I never . . .'

'. . . I never meant *hospi*' . . .'

'. . . never, flaming understood why she, called . . .'

'. . . *hospital*, Snow — I meant like, you know, some . . .'

'. . . called herself that! Eh? *What* then, the flaming, Home?'

'. . . somewhere, like, a *holiday*, Snow!'

'Cripes, cut it out, son! What, trip for two? To, *Fiji?*'

'Yeah, why not, Snow — you could . . .'

'Or, or that flaming Club Med? With, with a . . .'

'. . . you could take Snag, Snow . . . !'

'*What?*'

' — '

'What'd I, flaming, want to do, that, for?' Hah, ho!

' — '

'Come off it, Ike, that kid's, she's . . .'

'She's . . .'

'. . . she's just flaming, skin and bone, hah, mate — besides . . .'

'. . . she . . .'

'. . . besides, Ike, cripes, you know, she's young enough to be my flaming, I could be her . . .'

'. . . she bloody drives me wild, Snow!'

'. . . be her flaming father — *what?* What, her, you . . . ?'

'Oh Christ, Snow . . .'

'. . . you, flaming . . . ? Cut it out, she's just, skin and . . .'

'. . . I'm just this fat bugger with . . .'

'. . . she's just — Here, Ike, take it . . .'

'. . . just fatso with the bad breath!'

'. . . take it easy, Ike!'

'I could *care* for her, Snow!'

' — '

'Ever had kids, Snow?'

' — '

'What's up, mate?'

'You're flaming, pissed, Ike.'

'So're you. Can't even stand up. You old bugger.'

'You're flaming well, howling!'

'So, so're you, Snow!'

'She's a flaming, little goer, all right, Ike!'

'She's a cracker!'

Snow suddenly silent.

'Ah, shit, sorry Snow — I didn't mean . . .'

'Like, hell.'

'Go on, then, Snow — tell us the yarn about the cream crack' . . .'

'Get, stuffed!'

'Okay, don't. Tell us why you're bawling over Snag, instead.'

'God almighty, Ike — that flaming kid, she . . .'

'Spunky, eh?'

'. . . she — what? Nah, she — she reminds me . . .'

'When you was young and randy, when . . . ?'

'Belt up, Ike! Christ! She reminds me of, my flaming kid! The girl!'

'Your . . . ?'

'Be about that . . .'

'. . . your, you, your *kids*?'

'. . . about that, old, now, she . . .'

'You got kids, Snow?'

'. . . always was a skinny little — what? Whaddaya mean, "have I got kids?" What's, so flaming funny, what's . . . ?'

'I didn't mean — I mean, you never . . .'
'*Why the fucking, hell should I, talk about it!*'
'Okay, okay, don't get on your bike!'
' — '

'Take it bloody easy, Snow, you'll have a — *Jesus*, sit down
. . .!'
'Jus', forget it, all right, Ikey?'
'Whatever you say, Snow.'
'Ike, you jus' wouldn't, believe it.'
'"You're not going to believe this, but . . .", eh, Snow?'
'What?'
'Never mind — hey, d'ya, did'ja . . .'
'You gonna, flaming, chuck?'
'What? — nah, I jus' remembered, just reminded myself —
did'ja hear what Snag . . . ?'
'Belt up, about the flaming kid! Go on, Ike, give her a . . .'
'. . . what Snag . . . ? — wait on, Snow, this is . . .'
'. . . give her a flaming spell, Ike! Talk, about, something . . .'
'. . . this is different, Snow, this is . . .'
'. . . something *different* — eh?' Hah, heurp!
'. . . different — what? Yeah, I am, jus' listen, Snow. She . . .'
' — '

'. . . she — shit, Snow, *listen* will'ya? Did'ja, did she, the tank?
Did you hear about the bloody tank?'
'*Tank?*'
'Tank, Snow! Snag told us — that mad looking bugger with the
crook leg, nearly kicked you in the chops this morning, he . . .'
'At smoko?'
'That's the one! . . . he tried to get the boss to flog a tank for
him!'
'Get off it!'
'Didn' you, didn't you hear about it?'
'No one told me.'
'Didn't Snag tell you, Snow?'
Snow's trying to light a smoke.
'Told everyone else, you should'a heard the way she . . .'
'I'm, you . . .' Snow's trying to stand.

56

'You off, Snow? Here, let's . . .'

'I'm, flaming, off! — you, can't lay off, talking about the . . .',
hah!

'. . . let's give you a hand up — *Christ*, Snow, you . . .'

'. . . yakking on, about the flaming, kid!'

'. . . you better take it easy. Sorry, Snow.'

Snow stands up into the gritty wind.

'You all right? Snow?'

Snow's feet begin to walk him away.

'See ya, Snow. See ya tomorrow!'

' — '

'Get stuffed, then, crabby ol' bugger!'

Snow's silence, like an unfinished yarn, or an untold one,
'You're not going to believe this, but . . .' *nothing*! — the nothing
of his silence fades across the street past the time-switched
orange flashing of a pedestrian-crossing light, into the penumbra
of the deserted arcades, gone. In the distance, then, the shrill
howl of his cough — whinny, bark, and crow — horse, dog, and
cockerel — lone spirits of animals misappropriated by the city.

And at a tangent, Ike's heavy sad tread — heavy, and yet
dainty; as though, one day yet, he'll meet in the shadows that
invitation to dance with Snag beneath the stars.

12

EACH DAY *ANGKA LOEU* SPEAKS TO THE PEOPLE THROUGH THE broadcasts of Radio Phnom Penh.

Salvation watched the last warm tones fade from the sea. There advanced across its surface the dull armour of evening. A distant incandescence lit the cordillera across the Straits. Then it, too, faded. Nearby, the children of Island Bay were still clashing the metal chains of swings in the playground.

If you want to understand Vietnam, you have to understand the myth of Than Giong. That goes back to the tribal period of Old Vietnam, sixth century BC.

Salvation sat watching iron sheathe the sea. In the foreground, the headlights of cars swung their beams across his window. Silence fell in the playground. Three thousand years old, Than Giong still speaks to the people. But in Cambodia, Khmer, Kampuchea, it was *Angka Loeu* who spoke.

When the view returns nothing but the reflection of his own bearded face, Salvation draws down the bamboo blinds. He prepares rice. Salted slices of eggplant complete the meal still offered as a sacrifice to Than Giong. Giong's mother, an old peasant woman, became pregnant by stepping in a giant's footprint. At three, Than Giong had neither moved nor spoken. Then the king warned of enemies on the march. Than Giong called for an iron horse with a living heart, an iron rod, an iron hat. He devoured seven big bamboo plates of rice and three of salted eggplant. At Vuninh Mountain, a peasant army came to Than Giong's aid and the enemy was routed.

Salvation eats his meal which does not include fish. The phantom of a transaction in which his *please* had been followed by a *thank you* and by a pleasant dimming of the discordant traffic in black market PX items and even tins of New Zealand Kraft Cheese and bags of unacceptable milk biscuits — this melancholy phantom is appeased by Salvation's evening ritual in which he watches the fires of day sink and drinks whisky and thinks about the voice of *Angka Loeu* on Radio Phnom Penh.

The image of the three-year-old peasant child awakening from muteness to become a mighty warrior, aided by a peasant army, is the living symbol of a nation's self-defence. Salvation thinks about him as well as about *Angka Loeu*. The mandarin Li Te Xuyen gave Fu Dong Than Giong, the heaven-storming Holy King, the characteristics of a god of terror. People serving the Li dynasty were supposed to fear him. A ruling dynasty needs the Terror. But the peasants continue affectionately to offer seven bamboo dishes of rice and three of salted eggplant as a sacrifice to Than Giong, *their* Than Giong. And the terror of *Angka Loeu* that speaks each day to the people through the broadcasts of Radio Phnom Penh — is there a meal of rice to stop the voice of *Angka Loeu*? With eggplant that salt has drained of its fluid, as fear and pain draw off the fluid that tear-ducts offer to *Angka Loeu*? Where is the child in *Angka Loeu*, the child that calls for iron, an iron horse with a living heart, the people's friend?

Out the back in its shed is the M24 Chaffee tank which Salvation will visit later. Now he lifts the tender rice to his mouth with wooden chopsticks. Cambodia is a bowl surrounded by mountains. The talcose valley of Dien Bien Phu in Vietnam is also a bowl. Giants made it for their meeting place. The sound of their drums drowned out thunder. They competed in the building of mountains. They were the tribal forefathers. Their descendants, the settlers of the Red River Delta, Than Giong's people, knew the art of making bronze. With their great drums, they made themselves masters of the storms.

Now the Delta is a land of many bowls, of bomb craters that fill with rice. But the crater of Cambodia was full of smoke and the thunder of *Angka Loeu*.

Salvation sees the people walking through smoke. Some are pushing hospital beds whose castors are trapped by potholes in the roads. People are holding perfusion bottles above the beds.

He washes his dishes and sets the chopsticks upright in the bowl to dry. Whisky. The sporadic flash of headlights through chinks in the bamboo blinds tells him that out there, where the smoke of clouds might dull the clash of moonlight on the metal sea, the drinkers and movie-goers are returning to their unspoiled fishing village of Island Bay — their workaday caution a little excited, perhaps, by alcohol or some fantasy of daring. Beneath his mosquito net on the open verandah in Klaeng he'd nodded off allowing his eyelids to shutter down on the glimmer of kerosene lamps. When it came time to change the dressing on his leg, he'd lain back trying to stay in that trance for as long as possible before the first deliberate pluckings of the forceps lifted him up on his elbows into the fish-gut smell that came from beneath the pads of lint. His shuttering eyelids would animate the kerosene lamps along Klaeng's roadside stalls, where he never saw washing-machines, or the cast-out contents of grandad's shed, or deep-freezes; only the esoteric bric-à-brac of the crater-makers, plus army fatigues for giants; and once, climbing the mountain rim of the bowl that *Angka Loeu* had turned into an impenetrable barricade, he'd heard someone whistling the theme from *The Good, the Bad, and the Ugly* starring Clint Eastwood, and along the trail that could have been boobytrapped with claymores that only take your face off if you're lucky, had come this kid in black like a wraith of smoke, with pursed lips, whistling.

At some point the plucking forceps would dislodge his stubborn attention to a thought, and he'd open his eyes wide in agony and almost sit up. The theme music of *The Good, the Bad, and the Ugly* and the first of the Buddha's Four Noble Truths, Life is subject to suffering — and that's what comes of using your own name, your real name: you can't even tell where the evil spirits are coming from.

Khmer bandits, probably; gunrunners subsisting on monkey meat; smugglers who knew how to step through the *Angka Loeu* minefields, protecting their investment, and that kid was calling in the fire. Look, here comes one of them Clint Eastwoods! How was the kid to know it was only Salvation, call me Salvo, from Island Bay, New Zealand?

Call me any fucking thing you like, thinks Salvation — call me

Clint Eastwood, what difference does it make, did it make? As the smoke blew away he saw one of his Thai guides who seemed to be performing a cartwheel along the trail. The K-47 sounds different from an American Armalite, or a Kalashnikov or Dragunov. It sounds Chinese. For bandits and smugglers, these evil spirits were well provided for. It was the last burst of the K-47 that sent the Thai spinning down the track. Leaves and twigs were still spattering down all around as the smoke blew away, and there went the Thai, leg over hand, out of sight into the thorn bushes. *Angka Loeu* wouldn't have left it at that. Whoever it was that sent the kid down the track whistling 'The Good, the Bad, and the Ugly' wasn't waiting to see who else might show up.

And, *kids*? They were all Than Giong these days, Red Khmer version — *Angka Loeu* had them seconded to the Terror. A nation of children who were killers and informers. Walking out of the smoke.

The scar, like a railway track on a map, runs down the front of Salvation's skinny thigh, through an immense pucker above the knee that isn't there, and around to the middle of his calf, where it ends in another crater. The railway track itself is white and smooth. The indentations where its weals are raised in relief above his leg are purple. The craters or puckers are red. Where the kneecap's gone, the surface has a glossy sheen, as though covered over with gladwrap. Usually Salvation wears a metal brace. But if he walks on the leg too long, it seems to swell with blood.

When he first began to crutch himself about in Klaeng, prior to enquiring about a comfortable way to get up the Sukhumvit Road (Cardamom cordillera on the right, crocodiles and sharks on the left) to the British Dispensary and the Camillan Hospital but not the New Zealand Embassy, his first wee jaunt was to the roadside mart. At the sight of the Kraft cheese and the New Zealand milk biscuits there he began to laugh.

Nowadays, too, he no longer laughs at things because they're funny.

He's laughing now.

Time to visit his iron horse in its stable. Where it awaits its living heart. Its child rider.

The whisky, as he raises it toward his lips, refracts a tawny flash that reminds him of the red car that has caused him to hope that something interesting may happen tomorrow.

At night as he sleeps in Island Bay he listens to *Angka Loeu* speaking to the people through the broadcasts of Radio Phnom Penh.

'We are not here to laugh!'

— I'm not, he laughs, reappearing in the Chaffee turret.

Not here; not laughing.

Second Day

Second Day

13

THE MALE SPIDER IS SELDOM KILLED.

He stops and vibrates the web at intervals. If she continues to react violently, he will turn tail and run. If she remains passive he will reach forward with his front pair of legs and gently tap her. He then moves over her body until his abdomen is over hers and he is facing in the same direction. There seems little haste. The mating may be spread over half an hour.

After it is completed, the male moves leisurely away, resting at the margin of the web, where he usually begins to run his palps through his fangs and then later recharges his palpal organ.

She has a prominent red stripe. *Latrodectus katipo.*

He seems completely different — brown with a central black band.

'Are you recharging your palpal organ, Jackson?'

But Jackson is surly this morning. Wallace detects in him a mood of truculence. He peels oranges and bananas, piling the skins on his central black band. From kiwifruit, green juice runs into the black stubble on his chin. He has his dark glasses on, though sunlight cannot pierce the drapes across the portholes.

Early morning footsteps which would in the past have unnerved him, this morning made him curse under his breath as he gently tapped her. Then he moved his abdomen over hers while the steps advanced awkwardly down the wooden jetty — hesitated, came knocking back again, then left in the direction of the carpark. Something about them.

This wasn't someone sneaking around, thought Wallace. Sounded like cowboy boots. She was distracted from what Jackson was doing with his palps.

'Jackson?'

But now Jackson fangs a tree-tomato and does not respond. The pile of rinds and skins covers his stripe.

'Enjoying your breakfast, Jackson?'

He turns a glittering insect gaze upon her. Purple saliva drips from his mouth. 'Any juice?'

'In the fridge, Jackson.'

He rises, sweeping rinds to the bed, and slouches to the galley. She hears him tear the top from a juice carton, the prolonged gulping as he empties it.

'Jackson, that sounded like a cowboy on the dock just now.'

'Knock knock,' leers Jackson.

'Who's there?'

'De.'

'De who?'

'De police,' gloats Jackson, returning to loll among peels.

'Why, Jackson?'

Again the silence. Is this her Jackson, growing up? Moulting? Another surly repressive? After all she's done? Is this gratitude?

'What's up, Jackson? Tell Wallace.'

'Tell you what, Wallace? You know everything.'

'What's the matter?'

'You tell me, Wallace.'

'*Jackson*, you've moulted, darling!'

Jackson turns on one elbow. His warm fruit-salad breath is humid where he laughs in her face. Shreds of orange are packed between the superb teeth.

'Police, Wallace. That gorilla with the leg. Them women in a old van, hey? Well, they not watching *me*, Wallace. They watching you, baby. I done nothing!'

'Jackson, a breakthrough!'

'*Nothing*!'

'You have me to thank for this, Jackson.'

'For what?'

'For this new mood of . . .'

But Jackson has again arisen and is hunting among his clothes. Wallace witholds the word 'independence' from her sentence. Why give the lad ideas?

'Anything special you want, Jackson?'

'A swim.'

'A *swim*?'

'Eat fruit, swim, and fuck, Wallace.'

'But *Jackson* — how picturesque!'

'Getting the inside outside, Wallace.'

'No drugs, Jackson? No carwash?'

Fitting skants to his crotch, Jackson does not reply. His beautiful legs ascend the companionway. The launch rocks and Wallace hears the smash of water as he dives into the boat-harbour. Then comes the diminishing sound of Jackson swimming in the direction of the open sea.

My God, thinks Wallace. Overnight.

Related to the Black Widow, only the female *Latrodectus katipo* can sting. The classical age of so-called spider poisoning came in Italy near Tarento in the seventeenth century. Bitten by a wolf spider, a harvester would dance the tarantella, accompanied by roving fiddlers, hour after hour, until the poison was worked out. Special music was prepared. It was a profession. It had been a spasmodic (so to speak) craze for centuries.

Probably, the 'spider-bite' was just a front. Behind it, behind its nudge-wink, was the ancient cult of Bacchus.

This dancing mania revealed that the pagan spirit remained strong in the people through centuries in which they were encouraged to put the outside inside. The Church, the State, civilisation. Teachers.

Wallace listens for the swimming sounds of her returning pagan.

Envenomed by a radioactive spider, Spiderman becomes his insect totem. Too bad he has to be so drearily dutiful with it.

Dance, Spiderman, dance!

In the distance, Wallace hears the returning thresh of Jackson's limbs in the boat-harbour.

Among the effects of the female katipo bite are: cold sweats, increased blood pressure, rise in body temperature, anorexia, muscle spasms, priapism, insomnia, delirium.

Not bad.

Pain. But then, nothing's free, philosophises Wallace. Child-bearing is painful, too.

Oh, she's all we've got, with her beautiful red stripe. She's our only ally. She's the only one who can teach the children to dance!

After a minimum of six hours a day for twelve years putting the outside inside, and all those serums and innoculations of repression administered by the self-appointed guardians of the future, no wonder children grow up into monsters. Fearing the spider, enslaving the pet. Do you like my pussycat, shake hands with Fido, have a ham sandwich.

Above her head, Jackson hits the deck. Seawater precedes him down the companionway.

'Wallace, we go to the carwash!'

'Oh no, Jackson — I thought you'd come through!'

'Hey, not to do anything, Wallace, you know — just to check it out. Wallace, I feel great!' Jackson's chest heaves. A faint reek of diesel comes with the sea. He stands draining on to the cabin floor. 'I swum right out past them marina!'

'The *carwash*?' Wallace resists the urge to offer condescending congratulations. She feels suddenly lonely. Jackson's delight is so . . . normal.

'You'll see, Wallace,' grins Jackson.

'This has been sudden, Jackson.'

'Wallace, maybe just a leetle . . . ?' leaning ingratiatingly forward, dripping diesel sea upon her from his hair, pressing a forefinger beneath his nostrils. 'Because, you know, 's a beautiful day, Wallace!'

'A "beautiful day", huh?'

'*Beautiful*, Wallace!'

'That's my boy, Jackson.' That's better. Always something opportunist about the fast conversion. Don't change bookings just to get a ride on Fate. Fate is just another iron butterfly.

Now, that's pure *poetry*, Wallace commends herself, as she rises from the bed. She notes the involuntarily ingratiating movements of Jackson's eyes, unscreened by the Eastwood shades, as her russet-tipped breasts brush across his arm. She pauses a moment, there, to test him. Only Jackson's eyes are moving. Is he proving himself to himself, or to her?

Nothing is simple, dancing least of all.

Fate, is just somebody else's idea of the trip. That, Wallace, is survival arts. To hell with poetry. That's better, Wallace. Don't get sentimental.

Wallace glides past Jackson toward her larder of versatile venoms.

'Okay, Jackson. The carwash. We'll check it out.'

'Thank you, Wallace.'

See?

14

Oh save me save me
save me from myself
I'm the first to get trigger happy
first to think of my own hell

This morning Frank was in the front too. He was in a *we*. He had his elbow out the passenger window, he was singing.

Growls B.J., 'Don't you, you know, know any other songs?'

'Well I like it,' says Kate. 'You have to wear the buggers out, eh Frank? The good ones?'

We're in the front. *'Oh save me save me . . .'*

'This is mad, B.J., this is loopy, snooping on a Rub-a-Dub.'

'You started it, Katie. You know, you're the one . . .'

'. . . 'cause I'm whaa-ling,' happy Frank, *'out on the deep, just can't get used to . . .'*

'. . . the one who — *Frank*, you know, couldn't you . . . ?'

'. . . *sea, yes I'm whaa-ling . . .'*

'*Frank!*'

'What?'

'Let him sing, B.J. Sing your heart out, sailor boy.'

'Can't hear myself *think*.'

'Am I allowed to *whistle*? B.J.? Lieutenant?'

'Shit, Frank, do you have to get smart? You know, I just . . .'

'Ah forget it.' Frank slumps. 'Think I'm not used to it?'

It's sullen in the front.

'God, Frank, you know, *sing* if you want to, I didn't mean . . .'

'Why,' tries Kate, 'don't you just . . .'

'. . . put you down, you know . . .'

'. . . just leave . . .'

'. . . I'm sorry, Frank, you know, I just, I'm just . . .'

'. . . just leave him *alone*, B.J., Christ! "Don't sing", and then

70

it's "Sing!", don't you . . .'

'You know what . . . ?' sniggers Frank, as the J4 sidles past the downtown quays, '. . . know what . . . ?'

'. . . don't you — listen,' Kate persists, 'don't you reckon he's had enough being told what to do in his life, B.J.? Without . . .'

'. . . you know what I really like? Being . . .'

'. . . without *you* coming . . .'

'. . . being in the fuckin' *team*!'

'. . . coming at him as well? B.J.?'

'If it's any help to you two,' yells Frank, 'I'll get in the back.'

'Sorry,' says B.J., as though it meant not 'I am' but 'You will be'.

'I mean, I'm used to it B.J., just a reject. *You know*, a fuckin' refugee.'

'I'm sorry, Frank. I'm on edge, that's all. All this, you know, *drama*. As if this is what matters.'

'Oh no, no, no! It's *my* fault! Unwanted, *you know*!'

'Cut it out, you two,' Kate suddenly sounding tired or worse. 'Look, we're here. The Rub-a-Dub. What're we . . . ?'

'Well, you started it, Katie, you know, you're the one who chased after that red . . .'

'This is neat,' says Frank. 'Here we . . .'

'Better stop, anyway, B.J.!'

'. . . here we are, just like on TV, neat eh!'

But in the surveillance silence that's now come down in the hot, ticking van, where even Frank's scoffing snigger has been pre-empted by the vigil, it's Kate who feels she must measure her breath and muffle the beating of her heart.

Just like on TV. Another repeat. The perfect bodies. The children walking out of smoke.

Who are you?

You destroy me.

You're so good for me.

How could I have known that you were made to the size of my body?

You're great. How wonderful. You're great.

You're so good for me.

71

You destroy me.

You're so good for me.

Deform me, make me ugly . . .

Ahead, blurry Wakefield Street reticulates its mid-morning traffic through windy sunlight. You have to be ready for it, a receptive host, for this desolation to make your heart beat so, your breath come close to panting. Parked watching a carwash, for God's sake! All so serious, or something. And all she can think about is watching the world approach some speeding windscreen or other. It was always getting closer but it never came — years of sitting in clapped-out vans. The language of love that sounded like the language of disaster. And then the film running back the other way, the van's in reverse, little Jane's face left behind out there when she should have been getting closer — closer and closer, her lovely child smell, that perfect skin where her hair fell in a dark curl past her ear to her shoulder.

The way that woman had spoken in the Hiroshima movie last night — the things she said, while B.J. and Frank and her were . . . And the subtitles flicking over — her voice, smoke, the words on the screen.

And how sweet.

More than you can know.

The perfect bodies of the survivors, the lovers. The children walking out of the smoke.

Deform me, make me ugly . . .

'What do we do,' Frank hesitating with the 'we', 'when we . . .'

You destroy me.

'. . . when they, when it, if that . . . ?'

You're so good for me.

'. . . if, when that fuckin' Porsche shows up?'

Who are you?

'Deep-fry that sucker, right?' joshes B.J. 'Hey, God, look, Kate, what's . . . ?'

'No, I mean, do we — I mean . . .'

'Shut up, Frank — you know, look . . .'

'. . . I mean — what? Christ, I can't . . .'

72

'. . . look, Frank, Kate's . . .'

'. . . can't even open my . . .'

'. . . she's, Kate is *crying*, Frank! Katie, baby . . .'

'. . . open my fuckin' mouth without you jumping — what? What's . . . ?'

'. . . my baby, what's the matter, Katie, you know, what's . . . ?'

'Just leave me alone, B.J., Frank — it's just . . .'

'Hey *look*!' shouts Frank. 'It's here!'

'. . . I just — never mind . . .'

'Tell B.J., Kate baby.'

'You two! It's . . . !'

'Nothing, B.J., just a . . .'

'The Porsche!' Frank watches the red car slither into the Rub-a-Dub. 'It came! Kate, *Jesus*, don't . . . ?'

'. . . just like a kind of flashback, bloody *years* . . .'

'Hey! You two!'

'Just shut up, Frank, you know, let Kate . . .'

'Oh, fantastic,' says Frank. 'This is really fuckin' far out. This is . . .'

'I dunno,' says Kate. 'All those bloody years sitting in vans, farting around the place. My, Jane, Janie, over there. Maybe it was that movie last night, that French, those grownups with the smooth skin, and the kids walking out of the explosion — the smoke, their skin all . . .'

'I know, you know, baby, I know.'

'. . . all — *shit*, stop calling me baby, B.J.!'

'I'm sorry, Kate. Here, let . . .'

'Really, it's okay, B.J., now, I'm okay, I just . . .'

'You just . . .'

'. . . just couldn't . . .'

'You couldn't, you know . . .'

Kate's scream stops Frank's elaborate semaphoring at the Rub-a-Dub. 'Christ! Are you going to finish my bloody sentences, B.J., as well, or . . . ?'

'Oh, Katie, darling . . . !'

'Fantastic,' Frank observing the Porsche engulfed in the wash.

'I don't believe this. Now they're *both* howling. Listen, team, are we . . . ?'

'You drive, Frankie.' Kate's all at once grim — dry-eyed, her voice rough from weeping. She stares ahead at the carwash, its internal flicker of bright water.

'*Me?*'

B.J. looks up, sobbing, from the steering column. '*Him?*'

'Why not,' Kate reaching across incredulous Frank to open the door. 'The rest of us seem to have forgotten all about Mission Impossible.'

'What do I . . . ?'

'Just do it like they do on TV, Frank. Come on, B.J.'

'Oh Katie, you know, I just hate it when . . .'

'When you lose your grip, B.J.?'

'No, you know, when you . . .'

'Bullshit,' growls Kate. 'Here, come on, just . . .'

And as Frank scampers around to the driver's door, he sees the three loafers outside the auction mart up the road rise suddenly to their feet. It's that fat, and the skinny, the one that got called 'skeleton' yesterday . . .

'Hey, *look!*'

And now here comes the red Porsche, fast and clean, cleaving the sunlight.

15

SMOKO TIME AGAIN ON THE SUNNY FOOTPATH OUTSIDE Reliable Reg's.

'You're not,' wheedles Ike, 'going to believe this, Snag, but . . .'

'Cut it out, Ike. Can't you see ol' Snow's feeling crook?'

'What? — yeah, bloody well should be, too. No, but, *listen*, Snag . . .'

'What do you mean, "should be"?'

'What? — well, last night we was, we were both . . . Snag, hang on, will ya? — listen, *look* . . .'

'So, what do you have to tease him for, Ike? — that "You're not going . . ." . . . ?'

'I'm *not*!'

'. . . "you're not going to," etcetera — you know, why don't . . .'

'I'm not — look, Snag, Jesus, up there, up the road!'

'. . . why don't you pick on someone your own size, Ike? Ha ha ha, nice one . . . !'

But Ike's not fielding fat man jokes today. In wounded silence he observes the blue J4 parked up the road from the Rub-a-Dub.

'Aw, come off it, Ike — can't you take a joke?'

'Forget it, Snag.'

'Me an' Ike,' harp, hah, 'went on the, flaming piss last night.' Snow's face is grey under puce. 'Lay off him, Snag. He . . .'

'Hey!' Now Snag suddenly notices the J4 that's parked up the road. 'Hey, look . . . !'

'. . . he, y'know, he . . .' Snow managing an ill grin, elbowing Ike, '. . . he's, not quite . . .'

'. . . look, you jokers, it's . . . !'

'. . . not,' hoo, 'not quite, himself, eh Ike? In, flaming love!' hey, heurp!

Ike's big neck reddens humiliatingly.

'. . . it's — shut up!' yells Snag. 'Listen! It's that, those women from yesterday, that coughed up a grand for a freezer!'

'That's what I was trying to tell you, Snag!' — Ike seizing the diversion.

'The J4!'

'Yeah, Snag,' babbles Ikey, the blush making him sweat, 'the ones that . . .'

'I wonder . . . ?' Snag's beginning to. Something fishy in the atmosphere this morning.

'. . . the ones that give me the goory looks yesterday because I . . .' Suddenly downcast, soprano Ike does not wish to finish his sentence.

'Because you, flaming called Snag here "the skeleton"?' Snow's malevolent cheerfulness lifts his shoulders from the sunny wall. 'Go on, Ike — tell her it . . .'

'Aw, *Snow* . . . !'

'. . . tell her it's . . .' But Snow's leery eyes squeeze shut for the cough.

'. . . I wonder what those van people want?' Snag wonders what marvels might even so come down Wakefield Street despite the way the greengrocers' trucks are always there, and the trolleybus wires, and the long perspective down the street that way — where now the old J4 sits at the kerb with the three people yakking in the front seat; and the other way you can see the fire-station clock whose hands only move if you don't look. And pretend, go on pretending she can't see Ike's huge hands reaching out for her while they really help him eat a pie or something.

It wouldn't even cross your mind, and then you suddenly notice it: he's not taking the jokes, not making them, either. First things to go, that's jokes. And what about old Snow's dirty leer. 'I wonder what they're up to?' And the way she says that, she sees Ike hear it — his neck and face blazing, he's staring with desperation at the blue van by the kerb.

'. . . tell,' hahm, 'her it's, all right, Ike,' persists Snow. 'Go on, mate, nothing ventured, nothing, gained — you *like*, skinny . . .'

'I wonder . . .', wonder all you like: you'd have to be *really* thick not to get the hang of them — *men*, bastards, what is it that Aussie comedian says, 'Why don't you go and fuck your shoe?'

'You're not going, to believe this, but . . .', Snow's enjoying it, 'ol' Ikey here, he . . .' agh! 'Cripes, look at the flaming, colour of him!'

'*I wonder what they want, hey? Snow?*' And her tone's just right, they both hear it — Snow's grin packs up.

Silence. Downcast Snow lights another Sportsman. Ikey slurps from his can. The hands on the fire-station clock haven't moved, but it's almost past smoko — and then that red Porsche swoops across in front of them and smartly traverses the double yellow line down the centre of Wakefield Street, and slithers into the carwash.

She's seen it all before, yesterday for instance.

And it's the same sun that falls upon the wall where the sullen three rest their backs and look across at the woman like a burning cockatoo and the dark man like a film star with, today, a yellow golf cap on above the dark glasses, and what looks like a lopsided clip-on plastic moustache — the same light and the same heat as before, but now like everything else they've backloaded extra meanings. Aflame, ignited within the Porsche, the yellow hat and the red hair take the same light and heat into the carwash where they are known and treated with dispatch; but in there, they blaze in the midst of the water and the smothering rollers and tentacles, and emerge still burning.

The three outside the mart all stand gaping as the red Porsche flings glittering water from its windscreen. The faces in there are screaming weakly, as yesterday, but today Snag can *hear* them, and the dark man's turned his yellow hat brim-backwards and is making boxing gestures at the ceiling of the car.

Some people have to spend the long days typing lies into the boss's computer, recording bent deals; hearing their ordinary wisecracks bounce back off the worrisome facade behind which something extra's going on — someone with a tank, some women up to something, something about those people in the red car. And some people don't have to, seems like — like the bozo with the tank, the freezer women with a spare grand, the red car people.

And, what about men who just always get vaguely hassley, and you have to spend so much time slapping the thought of them away, or cracking jokes to slow them up — by the time you're finished with them and with the devious shit you're typing in for the boss (who'd rather walk out on it too but can't, it's a habit, like Snow's smokes that'll kill him just like business will kill the boss) — by the time you've done that all day every day, and never really had a clue about the other stuff that was going on just where you couldn't get to it — two people all lit up in a red sports car, or even a couple of lesbians with an old van and a spare grand — by the time you've spent the whole day fucking around with what you always have to, you could just say, 'Why don't you go and fuck your shoe?' to poor ol' fatso Ike there, and it'd come out so poisonous by then he'd probably drop dead!

'What, what was that, Snag?' — Ike's apologetic, puffy, fat-man voice.

'*I said, why don't you go and fuck your shoe!*'

The red Porsche with its cheering occupants swings wildly across the double yellow lines, flicking an arc of water like sweat from the secret parts of its chassis on to the asphalt, but Snag doesn't watch it accelerate away down Wakefield Street toward the blue J4. A few of her big sudden tears mark the footpath where she runs back into the shadow of the mart.

Guiltily shocked, conspiratorial, Snow and Ike watch her go, her high skinny shoulders lifted against shaking sobs. Their mouths hang open and silence comes out, like darkness — the shadow inside the mart, the muteness of clapped-out appliances, the mundane's silent pleadings for deliverance.

They don't see Salvation's tyre-smoking Valiant free itself from the clutter of greengrocers' trucks by the vegetable market and lock itself squealing into the wake of the Porsche. They're not interested in watching the blue old J4 execute a lumbering U-turn across approaching traffic and set itself to follow both. They don't see the chase diminish down the exhaust-hazed perspective of Waterloo Quay.

The fire-station clock says it's time to, but neither of them hurries to re-enter the smoky shadow. In there's the long-lost child of one, the impossible lover of the other. Dream of youth — dream of beauty. And they stand there in the wakeful daylight and feel like the deadly enemies of both.

16

JUST ENOUGH OF THAT 'BECAUSE, YOU KNOW, 'S A BEAUTIFUL day, Wallace!' stuff to put an aura around the words 'M24 Chaffee'. Wallace and Jackson do not stumble, but they pause. In full, the note by the companionway ladder reads:

> Got any use for an M24 Chaffee? Be at the carwash
> this morning.

'How do you do them *M24*, Wallace?' whines Jackson, his head beginning to swivel.

'I don't think they mean anything like *that*, Jackson.' Then Wallace is suddenly blinded. 'The footsteps!'

'A disguise!'

'Jackson, the footsteps! This morning!'

'My yellow hat! My . . .'

'On the jetty!'

'. . . my moustache, Wallace!'

'Your *what*?'

But in haste, Jackson descends the companionway. Now there is also the matter of the note. How could he have missed it when he went out for his — I can hardly say it, thinks Wallace. His *swim*. Just another brochure paradise.

'Got any use for an M24 Chaffee? Be at the carwash this morning,' she ponders aloud. She doesn't understand why, but this could be it.

Jackson's head emerges from the scuttle. It has a yellow golf cap on it, and a plastic clip-on moustache attached lopsided beneath the nose.

'Jackson, you look like Svengali or someone. Groucho Marx with dengue fever and a suntan. God, relax your *neck*, Jackson, or your head'll fall off.'

'Da bustache will.'

'Do I believe this?'

'What?' Jackson's nasal word swings past her as he swivels his whole body to scan the surroundings. The fisherman is there on his bollard and he still hasn't caught anything. A very beautiful jogger effortlessly bounds across the marina carpark with an immense foaming Rottweiler dog on a leash — she looks across at Jackson, and misses her stride. A man crosses the road from the chandler's with a coil of yellow nylon rope over his shoulder.

Rope? Dog? Fish?

'I'b dot geddink edythink, Waddace. Da dog, baybe?'

'Jackson, you missed the *note*, boyo. Couldn't you take that thing off?'

'Dote?'

'The footsteps, Jackson. They left the "dote", you dumb cluck — you didn't even see it, you and your total recall — Christ, you're a *sieve*, man!' Wallace whips the plastic moustache from Jackson's nostrils as he swivels stiffly past her to watch the Rottweiler's immense haunches pump their way through a gap in the trailer-sailers.

'Hey!'

'You can have the damn thing back at the carwash, Jackson, if it'll make you feel any better.'

'Not the carwash, Wallace!'

'You wanted it, Jackson.'

'But Wallace!'

'To prove yourself. To show you're liberated from it. I wonder . . . ?'

'But Wallace, these feetstops, this . . .'

'. . . wonder what's an M24?'

'. . . this letter, Wallace, them feets, they'll be . . . !'

'They'll be there, Jackson!'

'Who are "they", Wallace? Wallace?'

'" They" are who is getting in touch.'

'Who with?'

'With us, Jackson.'

'Why?'

'""They" have a Chaffee, Jackson.'

'What's a Chaffee, Wallace?'

'It's what "they" think we need.'

'Do we? Wallace? Wallace, do we need it?'

But Wallace has turned from Jackson's babble and is striding toward the Porsche. Trailing ropes of saliva, the Rottweiler's immense jowls re-emerge from the gap between the yachts, followed by the jogging woman. The fisherman's rod remains tentatively arched. The yellow coil of rope thumps to the dock next to a stack of sails and rigging. Jackson's not getting *anything* off this, zero, not a single top-line frequency, nothing with *meaning*.

'Excuse me,' it's the jogger, her perfect smile enlivened by panting, 'but aren't you . . . ?'

'*What*?' yells Jackson, and watches the Rottweiler's raw-liver lip shrink above huge teeth. Then Wallace is cramming him in to the Porsche. Then, sealed in, they back past the dog whose head comes nearly to the windows. The jogger's thighs strain to hold it from hurling itself upon the car. Jackson's primal yells buckle the air within. The fisherman has stood up from his bollard and the yachtsman with yellow rope pauses with one foot in his little dory. With a fling of loose gravel, the Porsche leaves them behind and joins the methodically spaced conveyance of traffic toward the city.

'See what I told you?' says Wallace soothingly as Jackson's lips once again sheathe his fangs.

'*Where*?'

'Back on full alert, huh, Jackson?' Today Wallace is satisfied with the normal progress, the regular flow. 'They're coming. They're beginning.'

'Who? What?'

'I told you, Jackson my boy. We don't have to do anything at first. They'll find us.'

'God, Wall' . . .'

'That may be expecting too much,' says Wallace drolly.

'Wallace, who will?'

'The people who need us, Jackson.'

'Who are they, Wallace? Wallace, who . . . ?'

'They'll be there. They'll be everywhere. Here, have your

moustache back, Jackson.'

'Dank you, Waddace.'

'I thought at the time,' purrs Wallace, delicately moving her car along its arterial cable toward prey, 'that your demonstration of independence this morning was just a little glossy, Jackson.'

Made shy by the moustache clipped to his nostrils, Jackson's smile is a stiff aperture within which his teeth crouch.

'Just a trifle tourist-brochure,' sighs Wallace. '"Eat fruit, swim, and fuck." I mean, *really*, Jackson. Where do you think we *are*?'

'Derely dere,' says Jackson. His smile remains locked tentatively in position, threatening ingratiation. Behind the dark glasses, his eyes swarm industriously over the evidence. 'We derely dere, Waddace.'

'That we are, my boy. The future remains magnificently ours to rediscover, Jackson. It belongs to us. Remember that, Jackson.'

'We dere.'

'Here we are.'

Swooping across the forbidden double line, Wallace aims the Spidercar at the dripping birth-chamber of the Rub-a-Dub. Jackson's laughter, bypassing the tongs of his false moustache, has never sounded more authentic.

'M24, Waddace!' he yells as the carwash welcomes them with cleansing jets. 'Chaffee!'

'Just for you,' cries Wallace.

'I didn' forgedt!'

'You never really do, Jackson baby!'

'*Daow*, Waddace! M24!'

17

'FRANK! TAKE IT EASY!'

'Woohah! Just like on TV, B.J., like Kate said!'

'Come on, B.J., now,' admonishes Kate, as the van flings itself through the town-hall traffic lights with only the battered Valiant between it and the Porsche. 'You're not driving, so be driven!'

'Kate, you know, you don't have to be sarcastic — this is no time . . . !'

'*Know* something?' Frank's peering ahead at the Valiant — he whistles in wonder.

'B.J., you think what's happening now's mad . . .'

'This, Kate, is no time to . . .'

'. . . if this is mad, tell me what's . . .'

'Youse guys,' driver Frank's locked on the Valiant.

'. . . no time to lecture me, Kate!'

'. . . what's — I'm *not*, B.J.! But just tell me, in your wisdom, if this is bloody mad, what's so straight-up-and-down about your freezer plan, all right, B.J.? If you think *this* is crazy?'

'You think it's crazy, Kate? You know, the freezer?'

'I'm listening to you guys,' whines Frank, 'but you're . . .'

'Come on, Kate — do you?'

'. . . neither of you's listening to me! Listen! That *Valiant* . . .'

'B.J., an All Black athletes' sperm bank's not a fucking Tupperware party!'

'. . . that Valiant — *what*?' quick as a flash, Frank — this time Frankie gets the lot, all the key words, on line: *athlete sperm bank* — they lock in place the way the three vehicles have, threaded on wire along Aotea Quay — Porsche, Valiant, J4. And Frank's bulging eyes are locked into that conga-line too as the Porsche selects the lane that will lead the dance to Lower Hutt; but he longs to turn off, into this conversation *here*.

84

'. . . Tupperware party, B.J., Christ! I mean, put politicians on the list, you know, diplomats, media stars, I mean, they can all *pay*, right?'

'Kate, you know, I think you . . .'

'Oh B.J., I'm just sick . . .'

'. . . I think you . . .'

'I *heard* you!', Frank wrenching the formation's tail up the motorway ramp past a patient queue of cars at a . . . 'Shit, that was a . . .'

'. . . sick of all this dumb secrecy bullshit, B.J., I mean . . .'

'Kate, I think you just, you know, told me where you stand!'

'. . . that was a police check-point, you guys. I hope . . .'

'Crap, B.J.! You know . . .'

'Just madness, right, Kate?'

'. . . B.J., you know very well where I stand!'

'Listen!' And it's Frank, now, yelling into the silence where the two women are staring into each other's tears. 'I am driving your van after the red Porsche, right? Listening? And in front that Valiant's also following the Porsche, right? Got that joker from the mart in it with the crook leg. All right? Now we all drove past a traffic check-point. Got that? The Porsche, the bugger in the Valiant and us. Meanwhile,' Frank's listen-with-mother inventory packing up, 'you, I hear you, you talking about sperm bank All Blacks? Right? *Freezer*, right? Am I right? Deep-freeze those suck', 'freeze those suckers, right? All chasing a fuckin' Porsche, one. Cops chasing us, two. Number three, you're sticking All Black nuts in a, in a . . .'

Through tears, Kate's and B.J.'s eyes are shining. Ignoring their forward propulsion, Frank's jabber, the windscreen's dusty frame of speeding billboards and blue sea, they move to kiss.

'I mean,' Frank's yells can't unlock him from the remorseless tracks of pursuit. 'I mean I'm used to just being the dogsbody round here. I mean I been used to it for years, haven't I! You know, do the dishes, that was Geek! — you know, get outa the way!' Unaccustomed to no interruption, Frank has begun to imitate B.J.'s hectoring style. 'Fuckin' drown, he wouldn't notice, fall off a mountain! I mean, whattaya want?', swiping his own

85

tears out of the way with a skinny forearm. 'D'ja rather get outa
the way outside with some hairy tossing you into rivers or inside
with a computer freak grabbing your balls? I mean, *drive*, big
deal! Go Frankie! Go for it Frank! We'll let ya! You're a-fuckin'-
llowed! All right? You know? B.J.? B.J., what's . . . ? Oh, wonderful, now they're climbing over the back!'

'Frank, you know, you're superb. And now you know
everything.'

'Kate?'

'Exceptional. It's okay, Frank. Just follow that Porsche. When
did you learn to shout like that?'

'But — what's *happening*? B.J.? Kate?'

The motorcycle cop passes smoothly by the driver's window,
making peremptory motions of the hand, cutting between the
Valiant and the J4. At the base of a billboard advertising beer for
a *man's* thirst, the formation breaks. The van idles in a cloud of
dust. Ahead, the red car and the Valiant drill their way through
the mirages that dance above the asphalt.

Get out of the car, learned that much.

Hello officer anything wrong?

That B.J., what a phenomenon.

Leave them to it, back there.

Was we meant to stop?

Oh, the tail-light. Yeah, the warrant of fitness.

All this time I fuckin' knowed she was up to something, the
bitch, but I never . . .

No I'm not the owner she's . . .

A *freezer*, B.J.!

She's, asleep in the back, ossifer.

Yeah I'm all right. Bit tired. *Officer*, sorry.

The other one? A friend.

No, travelling around. Nearly home.

Okay I won't wake them up. Thanks.

Ha ha, beauty sleep, yeah.

Yeah, warrant.

'Frank, you were superb.'

'Thanks, B.J.'

'You were so cool, Frank.'

'I'm used to them, B.J.'

'Frank, I'm sorry we . . .'

'You have to get a warrant, B.J.'

'Ha ha, what for, Frank? The . . . ?'

'The van, B.J.'

'Not the, not . . . ?'

'Not the freezer, B.J.?' Frank's face is not telling B.J. if this is a joke. 'B.J., I knowed you was up to something!' It's not.

'And now you know what.'

'Is it true?'

'We are going to ransom the, you know, sperm of famous athletes, Frank.'

'How . . . ?'

'Frank, you know, we are going to get some action, some basic . . .'

'But, how . . . ?'

'. . . very basic requirements are going to be met, or else . . .'

'. . . how, *you know*, how're you going to . . . ?'

'. . . or else, Frank, we start offering their precious, you know, sperm, in some very sporting locations, eh, Kate?'

'Operation Deepfreeze,' Kate's low chuckle.

'. . . how're you going to *get* it, B.J.? Off them. I mean . . .'

'It's a commodity, Frank. We control, you know, the means of production.' B.J. gloats at her joke.

'What if they won't?'

'Won't what?'

'Won't, hand it over, *you know*?'

'They can't refuse. Men never have. They never will. It's like, you know, taps.'

'Taps?'

'You turn them on.'

'What about the Porsche, then? The Valiant? Who're they?'

'Shit, don't ask me, Frank. Maybe they're just, you know, paranoid delusions.' This joke, too, B.J. relishes. 'Kate reckons they're cruising us, Frank.'

'And that's not all you don't know,' surly Frank setting the slow blue van to wander where the mad pursuit has long since gone.

'How's that, Frank?'

'Tell you what, B.J., if you know the answer to this question, I won't ask you the next one, all right?'

'What's up, Frank?'

'Here it is: why'd that traffic cop let us go, B.J.?'

'Maybe he . . .'

'Warrant a week overdue, broken tail-lights, you two pretending to be asleep in the back, he didn't even . . .'

'. . . maybe he was a . . .'

'. . . didn't even put a call in to the computer. Why didn't he, B.J.?'

'. . . a paranoid delusion. Maybe he was, you know, a nice fellow?'

'But they're not, B.J. They write tickets. *Nice*, shit.'

'Okay, Frank, fair enough. You know, it's your paranoia.'

'Well, I reckon you crapped out totally there. Now I get the other question.'

'If you must.'

'What happens to the kids?'

'Kids?'

'The kids. From the *taps*, B.J. That you're going to turn on. What about them, B.J.?'

From the far side of the cab, Kate's wide blue eyes looking across B.J. at Frank. Frank's bottom lip is wobbling. B.J. staring straight ahead, her shoulders humped up by her ears. She seems to blink as each approaching car speeds past her distant focus of vision. Frank's looking that way too, but seeing different stuff.

He hears Kate's dove-voiced *Aah* above the sound of transport powered by internal explosions.

B.J.'s voice is shaken by the engine beneath her. 'We, you know — you know, need to talk that through. I think we should all sit down together and, you know, talk the whole thing through. We should do that now. You know, as soon as we get back. We should all give each other the chance to go through it, to just, you know . . .'

Now Frank's turned from whatever it was he was seeing ahead. He's looking at B.J. as though she were a Martian — something fabulous, comical, and incomprehensible.

'Keep your bloody eyes on the road,' growls Kate gently. And with the same expression of incredulous derision, he looks back at where he's going — not just Lower Hutt, not any more, that's just prop-up junk. *This* vista he's never seen before: a bewildering miracle, brand-new, preposterous.

18

'Sɴ', Sɴᴀɢ?'

'—'

'Snag? You all, right?'

'Piss off you old bastard!'

'Snag, I'm sorry, here . . .'

'Piss off!'

'. . . have a, wipe with . . .'

'—'

'. . . here, use this, Snag.'

'That fat shit.'

'I thought you . . .'

'Thanks, Snow. Christ.'

'She's right, kid. Keep it.'

'Thanks, Snow.'

'I thought, you two, liked . . .'

'He's a pig?'

'. . . thought you, you was always . . .'

'Ugh, he makes me . . .'

'. . . but you was, always telling jokes, you two.'

'Oh yeah, ha ha, "the skeleton", ha ha?'

'Well, you give him, heaps about being . . .'

'Hey, listen, enough's enough, all right, Snow? I just . . .'

'. . . you know, you pour the, acid on about him being so flaming, fat and that.'

'. . . I just had enough, all right, Snow? Ugh, he was feeling me up with his eyes, right? You know, it . . .'

'He feels pretty . . .'

'. . . it just wears me out, Snow?'

'. . . pretty flaming, crook about it, about being fat, no one . . .'

'I mean, he's okay, he's nice really, he just . . .'

'. . . no one, crikey, no one's, no women, no girls'll . . .'

'. . . just, I don't like the way — *shit*, listen Snow, 's not my fault? What do you want me to do, fuck him just because he's . . .?'

'Hey, whoa, steady on, Snag, pipe down, we're supposed to be back, at flaming, work you know!'

'Bugger the work?'

'All right, forget I . . .'

Snag gulping tears in the penumbra of the warehouse.

'Snag?'

'Ah, shit, Snow!'

'Know what? You're on a, pig's back, really, Snag.'

'Don't give me that, don't, don't *patronise* me, Snow!'

'You're young, got a, good job . . .'

'Good job?'

'Yeah, what's . . .?'

'Call this a good job?'

'. . . what's, wrong, with it?'

'What's wrong with it, Snow, is I'm stuck in here all day flogging off dead peoples' . . .'

'Flaming pay's, not bad, the boss . . .'

'. . . old junk — *boss*? Him? He doesn't even know . . .'

'. . . he, if you'd seen as many, he could be a, lot flaming worse, Snag.'

'. . . doesn't even know there's a world out there?'

'He's got a business, to run, Snag.'

'Doesn't even get a buzz out of being offered a tank?'

'Tank?'

'Yeah, army tank? Didn't you hear?'

'Old Ikey may, have said something.'

'What would he know?'

'Just flaming lay, off him, Snag. He, likes you.'

'Slob — *likes*?'

'He, cares about . . .'

'*Cares*?'

'. . . cares, about you, Snag.'

'Big deal.'

''s true, Snag. He's got, a flaming, heart.'

'Oh yeah, thick as a wrist with a head on it like a calf's heart?'
' — ', haa, hoo!
'Shit, Snow, can't tell if you're coughing or laughing?'
'Bit of, both, Snag.' Hah!
'You need to take it easy, Snow?'
'That's what, they all, flaming, say.'
'Who all?'
'Ike, the other night, las' night, when we was . . .' Abashed again, Snow shuts up.
'You keep an eye on the slob, don't you, Snow?'
'We have, a beer.'
'You know, you should've been a sweet old grandfather, Snow.'
Hroar. 'Chr', Cherist Al' . . .'
'Snow? you all right? Want your hankie back? Snow? Here, take . . .'
Hah, heurp! 'Jeez!'
'Here, sit down, sorry, what . . . ?'
'She's right, Snag. I'm right, now. Stone the . . .'
'Did I say . . . ?'
'. . . flaming, crows, listen . . .'
'. . . I say something wrong? Snow?'
'. . . listen, Snag — you're not, going to flaming, believe . . .'
'Steady on, Snow, no time for . . .'
'. . . believe this, but . . .'
'. . . lay off, no time for jokes, now, Snow?'
'. . . you're not, going to believe, this, but,' hah!
'Get your breath back, Snow, here . . .'
'You're, not going, to believe this, but, I prob'ly *am* a . . .'
'Hey! Somebody?'
'. . . prob'ly, *am* a, flaming . . .'
'Oh shit! Ike! Over here, quickly!'
'. . . a, flaming gr', grandfather!'
'Oh God! Ike!'
'What's up, Snag?'
'Old Snow here, the old bloke went a bit blue, he's . . .'
'What'd he . . . ?'

92

'Go on, Ike, don't just — ring the ambulance, shit!'

'. . . what'd he, what was he talking . . . ? Okay, yeah.'

'You right, Snow?' Snag crouching where Snow sits on the dusty concrete floor.

' — '

'You just sit tight, we'll get some oxygen into you?'

'Sn', Snag, listen — you could,' hah, 'could, be my, you could . . .'

'Hey, it's all right, Snow, just . . .'

' — '

'That's right, just . . .'

'You, could be, my flaming . . .'

. . . when it comes in like a dream it can be so . . . sweet. You know, how the kids used to wear them sunhats with the Foreign Legion flaps down their necks? It could break your heart, to see them running in the sun in their hats — you wanted to say, don't fall over, you kids, your hats won't help you! Only made of towel, see?

Running on the back lawn in summer, when it was all dry and brown it was like they was in the desert. That was what it reminded you of, specially with the kidlings in them Foreign Legion hats. Caps. His was blue, hers was yellow. The sprinkler down by the strawberries would chuck glittery water, they'd run through it.

Of course, never saw any Foreign Legion in the desert, but the blokes used to hang a handkerchief down behind their helmet. Then there was that Laurel and Hardy picture, where they was in the Foreign Legion. Remember where they was all walking in a sandstorm holding each other's rifles, only the front of the squad got hooked up to the back so the whole shebang tramped round in a circle? Then the bit where they threw brass tacks all over and opened the gates of the fort. The way them barefoot Arabs hopped! Laugh!

Well, that was the only place I ever saw Foreign Legion caps.

Funny how it just breaks your heart — it seems to be happiness watching the little snooks there under the sprinkler, but then you think, what's going to happen?

Them Foreign Legion hats made it worse, somehow, could you believe that, Snag? You wouldn't believe it, Snag, the way the wife performed when she found out what I done to the hats.

Found bits in the incinerator, and when I tried to explain about the Foreign Legion you'd have thought she was dealing with a flaming nutcase!

Other thing was, down the edge of the street in winter the ice set in the gutters. It used to fair give you the creeps to see the boy on his bike whisking out there. It was only a cut the day that car collected him, but you should've seen the way the blood run down over the driver's white shirt when he carried him in, all floppy. Couldn't hardly blame me for what I done to the bike after that, though the kid was wild about it. But she laid on a dingbat of a performance, topped everything she'd done lately!

Bad to flaming worse, Snag, you wouldn't believe it — couldn't hardly follow what was happening. When you go on the piss sometimes, it's because it stops the happiness changing into the other.

She always was a skinny little thing, like you — come to think of it, the boy'd be about the same age as Ike, bit older maybe, hope he didn't turn out that fat.

You shouldn't be hard on him, Snag, he thinks you're Christmas. I mean, suppose he'd been born like me, too flaming good looking for his own good, hah? What good would that have done him?

Ike, you wouldn't believe how it can break your heart just not to ever see them. And then the bitch told the flaming law I'd been hanging about chucking stones on the roof. Why'd she do that for? Was that what she thought of me?

You wouldn't believe it, don't know how lucky you are, Snag — all them poor buggers, maintenance men, at Kinleith, Hillcrest work-camp, flaming slave labour, turn your pay over to the work-camp cop and piss up on the rest.

It's them Foreign Legion caps I remember, Snag — funny, eh? Them, and the sprinkler water like in the desert, and the bloke's shirt all red. The kids! And they got this idea of me standing outside the flaming hedge chucking stones on the roof!

I can remember that happy feeling watching them on the back lawn, Snag, and if I stop it there before it turns into that kind of worry about the hats being no flaming use, then I can just about imagine they're your kids, Snag — the girl's, or young Ike's there.

Guess she just got sick of me hitting the flaming bottle. Couldn't help it.

Mad, eh. As if they could be my kids, and you, and your kids, and their kids, all at the same time, and you haven't got any even, and I don't know if she has, or him. Flaming *Gran'dad*, eh?

Mad as a meataxe, I reckon, just like they said.

Blue and yellow, the sprinkler whizzing around by the strawberries, I can bloody near see it now. But then it all went up in smoke, anyway. What the hell do you do about that? No flaming use going on and on about it. Too late.

Ha ha, just have to hope she didn't turn out too skinny or him too fat, and that they both stayed on the happy side of things, would that be about right, Snag?

Ah, never mind about fat or skinny, just so long as they come out on the happy side of things — would that be about right, Snag?

Snag?

Snag?

'Snag?'

'Here I am, Snow, take it easy, we're nearly there.'

' — '

'They're looking after you, Snow. Don't worry, Snow.'

19

'WALKS IN THE SUN' WAS WHAT THE FREE WORLD MILITARY Assistance Forces in Vietnam used to call it.

That meant the Americans. The mean little South Koreans Salvo didn't think about. The Australians and New Zealanders he could not readily forget, though he tried. Seemed like he'd walked out of the smoke with nationality erased from his body, the way a claymore took your face off if you were lucky.

Only took your hands, feet, and balls off too, if you were lucky.

'You are not here to laugh.'

— I'm not, laughs Salvation. From the turret of his old automatic Valiant he watches the Chinese greengrocers scurry about with crates of cabbages on trolleys. They have loud New Zealand accents.

When he closes his eyes, he's pretty sure he knows where he is. When he opens them, he's not so sure. The greengrocers have hands, feet and faces, and, presumably, balls as well.

In his wing mirror he can see the Rub-a-Dub. Sunlight splashes across emerging vehicles. Over the road is the auction mart which makes Salvation laugh also but not because it's funny. Twin Cadillac V8 engines in the Chaffee, only 220 hp SAE but it would drive through those loading-bay doors and the interior stacks of junk as though nothing was in the way. Plenty of room in the turret with that concentric recoil system. The 75 mm M6 gun was for playing snooker — cannon out of the Mitchell bomber, it could pot rounds into the drawers of that twerp's desk inside, you'd see the clapped-out appliances flying out the windows and the interior lit up for just a moment by illumination that resembled sound — its glare made your teeth jump in their sockets.

What're *they* looking at? thinks Salvation — Haven't they seen anyone laugh before?

From their flat-bed trucks, stacking gro-paks, the Chinese greengrocers watch Salvation. He watches them back, sometimes closing his eyes and laughing, and always when he opens his eyes again the first place he checks in the wing mirror is the Rub-a-Dub.

'A walk in the sun' was what the Americans said you took when someone'd told Charlie you were coming. Would the Porsche come? In his mind's eye he sees it yesterday evening dive like a line of tracer through the dusk and down among the rows of trailer-sailers. He remembers it yesterday morning driving out of the carwash into the gap between a big red bus and a Holden ute — his leg aches as memory helps him flick the Porsche out left away from contact.

Free will was what Charlie believed in — that and the Chinese combat doctrine of Mao Tse-tung: When the enemy advances, withdraw; when he defends, harass; when he is tired, attack; when he withdraws, pursue.

You 'went for a walk in the sun' because Charlie Cong liked to choose. He also believed in 'one slow, four quick'. 'One slow' is when you prepare and rehearse — slow, slow. Slow as those evenings after the sun's fallen into the Gulf and you've nodded off after your '*Dai prod?*' has scored you a '*Khob khun*', and you can barely hear the racket down the road where they're flogging American PX, or is it the kids clashing iron in the Island Bay playground after the sun's gone behind the cordillera across the water with its evening armour of dapple camouflage?

Slow, slow, slow. And then *fast* from a secure place: one fast. Assault quickly: two fast. Clear the battlefield quickly: three fast. Withdraw quickly: four fast.

You wouldn't even see them, just smoke walking back into the smoke, and that Thai still cartwheeling at the end of the K-47 burst.

But that was in the Cardamoms. It was gunrunners or jewel prospectors, monkey-meat men, they could fly over Angka Loeu claymores, they'd stopped listening to Radio Phnom Penh, they were *nowhere*.

Salvation closes his eyes and listens to the Chinese greengrocers argue about the second leg of the TAB double. Slow, slow. This morning, a slow walk in the sun. Awkwardly down the decking of the jetty. A fisherman there on a bollard — his will to catch fish had not impressed Salvation.

So much the better. One fast. Contact. He scribbled, 'Got any use for an M24 Chaffee? Be at the carwash this morning.' Inside the launch he could hear them screwing.

'You must be fuckin' outa ya mind, that Lazy Boy's jus' *dogfood*,' Chan's Fruit and Veg, Kilbirnie, is shouting and banging crates of butternut pumpkins on the back of his truck; and when Salvation opens his eyes, he sees another smiling Chinese face staring in via the wing mirror, really close, but behind him the red flash of the Porsche entering the Rub-a-Dub's luminous spray. Ah!

Two fast? *Now?*

Reaching to switch on the twin Cadillacs and engage the hydromatic transmission, Salvo's fingers find instead the keys of his Valiant, while a hand through the window detains his arm.

'Here, hang on a minute, mate?' It's the Chinese face from the mirror. 'Wait on?'

And the Porsche has gone. Like tracer gracefully through a rainy fringe of trees. Don't lose it. Two fast, assault. Keep the momentum — you'll be smoke walking in smoke, *nowhere*. You'll be Than Giong, the child's heart in the M24 Chaffee, swing that M6 across and down, make thunder, make smoke.

'What the fuck do *you* want, Charlie?' got a face like that Lai Huu — smokewalker started out with Viet Minh *maquis* — after the French Expeditionary Corps' Trinquier started running bandits around with opium revenues, Huu walked out of the smoke into Binh Xuyen pirate concessions in Saigon-Cholon, lower-echelon power-broker loyal to Binh Xuyen pirate leader Bay Vien, emperor Bao Dai, and the anticommunist French, in that order — hard at work learning how to take tanks to bits, M24 Chaffees the French inherited from the Americans after World War Two — his smiling face not unknown in Saigon-Cholon as he made sure Binh Xuyen opium dens were sufficiently protected — walked out of the smoke again in 1955 when the French Deuxième Bureau and the American CIA were waging proxy war in Saigon-Cholon with pirates on the French side and Prime Minister Ngo Dinh Diem's ARVN on the Americans' — there was smokewalker Huu the Smiler in a Chaffee turret —

'Listen, mate what ya parked here all morning for laughing?'

— walked out of the smoke again when Diem was assassinated in '63, ended up stuck like a habit to Nguyen Van Thieu, by now he could fix M24s with chewing gum, bailing wire, and banana stalks —

'You know, we're busy round here, hey!'

— even American advisors from the Fort Knox Armour School knew about Huu ('Who?' was the way the joke went) but when they phased out the Chaffees for Walker Bulldogs, Huu was still smiling; and the Chaffees that were meant to be immobilised as pillboxes didn't all get to their final destinations — 'Coup Troups' was what they called the ARVN armour, the tanks were 'voting machines' — Huu smiling — tanks put Diem in and took him out, they put Khanh in and took him out, put Thieu in and protected him from flyboy Ky; and when the Americans left with their heroin habits, there was smiley Huu with his heroin fortune and a lineup of M24s, *souvenirs*, only he didn't wait for liberation, his smokewalking ways were too well known by then, he'd moved his iron horses to Cambodia —

'We got to *park*, you know? Hey?'

— along with plenty of Armalite AR15s, Chinese Type 56s, Russian SKS carbines and Kalashnikovs and Dragunovs, North Vietnamese K-50Ms, Chinese Pistol Type 51s —

'You know, someone might drop something on you, fella!'

— Soviet Tokarev TT33s, Heckler and Koch PSPs, US M1911A1 Colts, and even those South African Mamba 9 × 19 mm parabellum pistols!

'You know, this is a workspace, hey!'

'What the fuck do you want, who,' ha ha ha, '*Huu* are you?'

'Listen, this is a *vegetable market*, mate! You crazy?'

And when *Angka Loeu* walked out of the smoke and into Phnom Penh in '75 and started burning the books and all the paper money too, Huu was already across the border in Thailand with all *his* paper and plenty of gold as well; and his souvenirs, warehouses of them, and the old Chaffees that still made him smile like a monkey-meat man, a bandit in a white sharkskin suit, smooth and white, like a plump bag of Double U-O Globe Brand heroin!

'And you call *this* a market?' — and scoffing Salvation reaches forward and turns on the twin Cadillacs, ha ha; and Huu-face isn't laughing either as Salvation backs the Valiant among the trolleys and trucks, and then revs forward in a cloud of rubber smoke past the angry shouting greengrocers — just in time to see the Porsche dart out of the carwash.

'. . . too fast!' yells Huu and hurls a leek at Salvation's window.

— Damn right! On fire from hip to toe, Salvation's using the braced leg to gun the Valiant down Wakefield Street.

'Two fast!'

20

'TELL YOU WHAT, IKE, I COULD DO WITH THE AFTERNOON OFF after that lot?' Snag's voice wobbles across the words, the bridge over the torrent of her tears.

'Is he . . . ?'

'I thought he was going to croak, Ike, right there?'

'What're they . . . ?'

'They wheeled him off into a lift, I couldn't go. Poor old bugger? He kept coming half-way round and then his eyes would turn up all white, must've been a heart attack, Ike?'

'You should ask for the afternoon off, Snag, you didn't ought to have come back, you . . .'

'From *Reg*? You must be . . .'

'. . . you don't look too good yourself, Snag.'

'. . . you must be joking — time off from Reliable Reg?'

'Reckon you should ask, Snag.'

'He wouldn't even take the afternoon off for his *own* heart attack!'

'He'd have one just thinking about it!'

Ike's soprano giggle, Snag's cackle.

'Poor ol' Snow, Ike — he kept on trying to say, *You're not going to believe* . . .'

'*You're not going to believe this but all you need's* . . .'

'. . . *believe this, but* — what?'

'. . . *all you need's a Huntley and Palmer cream cracker.*'

'What, Ike?'

'That's what he . . . this joke he . . .'

'Wasn't a joke, Ike, not this time?'

'No, whoa, I didn't mean . . .'

'He kept trying to say something about kids, Ike?'

'. . . I didn't mean he, you know . . .'

'Ike, it was when I said something about he should've been a

101

sweet old *grandfather*?'

'. . . didn't mean he was telling you a, you know, he's never finished that weka yarn — what?'

'. . . he should be a grandfather because — *Jesus*, Ike, will you stop rabbiting on about . . .'

'He should be a grandfather?'

'. . . about Snow's weka? — Yeah, I just said that,' Snag licking at fresh tears, 'it sort of slipped out — like, he's so kind, you know, and . . . shit . . .'

'Yeah, he . . . aw hey, come on, Snag — hey, you want me to ask the boss if we can . . . ?'

'He's so kind, Ike? And so lonely, you know — it's like *we're* his kids or something? I mean, he doesn't even . . .'

'Snag, he's . . .'

'. . . doesn't even, I mean, he lives all by himself somewhere up . . .'

'. . . he's got, Snag, he told me the other night . . .'

'. . . an' when I said that? About being a grandfather? That was when he went all blue, Ike — I mean, it was like it was *my* fault? I shouldn't, shouldn't have, shouldn't . . .'

'Whoa, steady, hey, come on, Snag, we're going, come on out for a walk, or I'll take you home or something, fuck the boss.'

'Ike, it was like what I said about kids just turned a switch off in him? It was terrible, he just . . .'

And without surprise, Ike sees his own fat arm fold itself about Snag's wretched shoulders. He can feel her tiny bones shaking under the denim jacket that might as well be on a coat-hanger it seems that untenanted — but Ike can feel Snag's skeleton rattling in there as though it might fall apart, his big arm holding it together.

And so's Snag, at first, stiffly keeping her distance from him. But then she turns and leans her head down against his breathing soft breast, he's looking at her spiky hair and the pale scalp beneath, the knobs where her thin neck goes down into the too-big jacket.

'Come on, Snag, let's get out of here.' He walks weeping Snag past the boss's office. Reliable Reg's mouth is furiously opening and shutting by a telephone in there, can't hear what he's saying, they don't stop to listen.

On a park bench by the Port Nicholson yacht marina, Snag blows her nose into Ike's hanky and stares ahead at the wobbling masts of yachts. It was the way Snow'd been looking for her when he came to in the ambulance, and then his eyes had rolled back again — that look had reached right into her and gripped her tough, ordinary-sized heart, and made it stop for a moment while she kept hearing her own voice saying the words that had switched Snow off — *you should've been a sweet old grandfather.*

A man in a pram dinghy is sculling out through the marina, a smell of marijuana comes from a group of idlers with their shoes off by the bushes at the far end of the little park, and with puffy eyes Snag can also see a few high slow little clouds advancing across a blue sky where gulls circle in the glare.

A beautiful day.

Seems like it's an endless holiday out here — 's got flash red cars and tough women with extra cash and that bozo with a fuckin' *tank*; but on the inside, like it was a different world, there's poor old bloody Snow looking like he never had a holiday in his life, and the last thing he wants to do before they cart him off, is see *her*.

'How ya doin' now, Snag?'

'Not too bad, thanks, Ike?'

And on the outside, or on the other side, was this world that didn't even seem to be on the same planet!

''s not, not *fair*, Ike!'

'It's a bastard, all right.'

And sometimes you felt as though you could just walk out into the other one — like, walk out through a door and just into it, with nothing in the way — not Dad's boozy breath then, or bloody work, or that thing you felt like with Ike's hands whenever he looked at you, hands coming out of his eyes. You needed to be small, like with one side only, so you could turn yourself into an edge and just go through crowds.

'Sorry, Ike, don't worry about me — we should go in and see him some time soon, us two?'

103

'Yeah, we should find out . . .'

Between them Ikey can feel again the barricade of Snag's anger or whatever it is — 'we' sounded wrong, both times. She sits there stiffly as though ready to leave. But she stays.

Maybe he should go. 'Maybe, Snag, I should get back to work, tell the boss you . . .'

'Don't worry about it, Ike — I'm sorry if I . . . I mean, thanks for looking after me, eh? You know, getting me out of there? I'm sorry if I'm mean to you, Ike, I just . . .'

'Doesn't matter, Snag. It's all right.'

'You know, we can still have a laugh, Ike? Ike, you know what I mean?' She watches his fat fingers wring at each other. 'Ike, I'm really sorry about what I said before.'

'What was that, Snag?' His funny piping voice, pointed away from her.

'You know, when I said go an' fuck your shoe?'

Ike raises one fat grubby foot. ''s only a jandal, Snag.'

Their laughter frightens the gulls perched along the railings by the water. The loungers by the far bushes look up and see the big fat joker and the skinny punk awkwardly hugging each other, like children acting parts. They they're tussling over a jandal. The girl slings it into the marina and runs jeering to the foot-path. The fat man ambles past, whacking the remaining jandal against his immense thigh, a goofy smile on his face.

'Hang on, Snag . . . what I was going to tell you — hey, wait on?'

'Don't you,' wary Snag, 'whack me with that thing, Ike?'

'No, there's one more . . .'

'This is a trick, Ike, I'll . . .'

'. . . there's one more *serious* thing, Snag, about Snow — wait on, will ya?'

'No tricks?' Snag's shoulders, stiff, up by her ears.

'Cross my heart, Snag. No, listen — jeez, stand still, will ya? Listen, I was going to tell you just now . . .'

'It's about Snow?' Her stiff face.

'That's what I said — *Listen*, Snag, will ya?'

'Ike, if it's something . . . if it's stink news, Ike, like I don't want to know, all right? I've had . . .'

'No, it's — what do you mean, stink?'

'I've had enough monstering for one day, all right?'

'Jus' shut up and listen, Snag, stand still, will ya?'

Her red eyes on him, her shoulders humped up.

'Last night we had a few beers, Snow and me, and we . . . we, was talking about you, Snag . . .'

'Shit!' And Snag's all set to go.

'. . . and — *wait* — ol' Snow — jus' *wait on*, Snag — ol' Snow said, you made him think about his daughter, his kids, I . . .'

And her mouth flies open.

'. . . I didn't even know he had . . .'

'Ah, *no!*' Snag, wailing.

'. . . he had kids, you know — if he, you know — I mean, we should try to . . .'

She's jammed the knuckles of one hand in her mouth.

'. . . we should try to find out, Snag?'

'He said that? Me?'

'Yeah, Snag, he just said you made him think about . . . he was pretty pissed, Snag, he got kind of worked up . . .'

'Yeah? And what about all that bullshit out there on the footpath at smoko, Ike? Hey? Think I didn't get that? You two having a bit of a giggle? Think I don't know what all that was about? *Talking about me?* Listen, fatguts, you jus' . . .'

'Hey, whoa!'

'. . . just, both,' Snag shrieking, 'leave me *alone!*'

'But his daughter, Snag . . . he, his kids, you . . .'

'Jus' *fuck off!* Think I don't know what that's all about? His *daughter!*'

'*What if he dies, Snag?*'

'What?'

'What if he dies . . . you know, his . . . ?'

'Who cares.'

'*Jesus*, Snag, what's . . . ?' And now it's Ike's turn suddenly to blubber, his big bottom lip hangs out of his cheeks and he stands there with an old jandal in one hand and shakes his fat shoulders and belly, his flowing eyes just staring at little Snag's ferociously alert face, her mouth that almost seems to have bared teeth, the rage of her chalk-white nostril rims — 'What's . . . ?' — just stands there helplessly bewildered as though he might as well roll over and offer the soft vulnerable throat and belly that now gulp and heave with sobs that block the words that might . . . 'Snag, I . . .'

'Aw, you're all the bloody same,' says Snag, 'young, old, fat, skinny,' but without conviction now, because she knows what's coming — she's already heard it.

'Not Snow,' Ike wiping up with the hanky that's already wet with Snag's tears. 'Maybe me — yeah, me, all right, Snag? I could go for you, you're . . . But not, not old Snow. You remind him of . . .'

'You already said that?'

'Well, I can't help it, can I, Snag? If you, you know, turn me on? Doesn't mean I'm going to do anything!'

'Fat chance, Ike!'

'That's right, fat . . .'

'Fat chance!'

These tears that turn into laughter, this laughter that is like weeping, these jokes that hurt and save — these survival arts balanced above half-told secrets, these fangs and fears, these doorways for escape and capture . . .

'Jesus, Snag, I can't keep up with you, mate. One moment you're all upset over poor old Snow there, the next . . .'

'You wouldn't understand, Ike? It's nothing to do with you.'

'Fair enough. We better get back.'

'I reckon.'

Ike's walking with one jandal on. It stops him looking sad.

'Sorry, again, all right, Ike? Bit of past history, that's all?'

'Forget it.'

— *How, Ike?*

21

ON THE OPEN VERANDAH OF THE HOUSE NEXT DOOR, AN OLD white bull-terrier is walking round and round in staggering circles trying to get at his backside. From time to time he slumps to the worn boards and lays his immense scarred muzzle across one paw.

This he does as if in parody of his owner who emerges every half hour or so from the dim house with its television voices, and pumps a 5 kg barbell — wrist, forearm, bicep. The man's grunts of exertion conceal a sexual subtext somewhere, while the raised and lowered forearm involuntarily repeats a semaphore of erections.

Ten each side — and then the man slumps with his big squarish belly across the verandah balustrade, his thick dark shoulders beaded with sweat. Soon, he will return to the obscure interior where, sporadically, a woman's voice rises in song or argument.

'Bet you didn't know,' angry Frank's clever dirty fingers busy disconnecting the internal parts of the freezer, 'but that guy over there's a famous athlete.'

B.J.'s watching Frank as though to memorise his moves.

'B.J.? Know that? 'Course not.'

'Frank, we think you're over-reacting.' Kate's greyed head is turned toward the thickset athlete leaning across his balustrade. 'Who said anything about . . . ?'

'If I don't believe you, will they?'

'Will who, Frank?'

'The fuckin' *athletes*. The *All Blacks*.'

'You're on the inside, Frank, it's different.'

'Okay, Kate,' Frank's fingers pause, 'suppose you hop over the fence and get some off that guy over there. Middleweight finalist, Commonwealth Games Christchurch. Mind you, you'd have to have a word with his old lady first. Then you'd have to get his pants off.'

Over by the dusty window, Kate's lean shoulders have begun to shake. She's looking at the middleweight's old pig-dog walking around after his own arsehole, the boxer swelling with exertion. 'We had something more newsworthy in mind, Frank,' she says, quickly, before laughter. 'God, *look* at him!'

'He's after a comeback,' says Frank. 'What would *you* know — he's got a following of thousands. This rich businessman once set him up in a training camp in the States, after those Games. He went professional. Geek even sent me to one of his fitness clinics once. All day until you got black spots in front of your eyes!'

'Frank.' B.J.'s patient tone. 'Let's, you know, do some work on this problem.'

'Here we go,' Frankie's Phillips frees the cowling above coils of gas-reticulation pipes. 'Here it comes. The B.J. lecture.'

'Just listen, Frank. You know, stop for a minute.'

'Not on your life.'

'But if you don't believe us, you know, why wreck the freezer?'

'I'm not wrecking it. You want it to go again, you just have to ask me.'

'But, you know, *why*, Frank?'

'Because, B.J., the only thing that'd make me believe . . .'

'Let's, you know . . .'

'. . . me believe — shut up — only thing'd, if I was a, *famous athlete*, shit . . .'

'. . . you know, let's *talk* Frank?'

'. . . if I was a — *talk*? You mean listen, B.J.!'

'I mean, we never talked about it. You know, you just . . .'

'*Never talked*? Christ, B.J., you never told me fuck all! Except shut up!'

'Okay, Frank, you know, I'm sorry, but now . . .'

'Now I'm on to you, you want to *talk*! Well, it's . . .'

'You just tore home, Frank, you know, started taking the freezer to . . .'

'. . . it's too late now, B.J.!'

'. . . to bits, you know, didn't even give us a chance to . . .'

'Frank,' Kate over by the window, 'Frankie, come and get a look at this.'

'Why?'

'Because we're not stupid, that's why, Frank.'

'Ha ha.'

'Listen, if you . . .'

'Don't *you* start telling me to . . .'

'. . . if you . . .'

'. . . telling me to listen as well, Kate!'

'. . . if you — what? I'm not, Frankie. I'm just trying to say — say if you were trying to score a cigarette, who would you, who'd you used to ask, Frank?'

Frank watches her, sullen and alert.

'You'd ask someone you thought would give you one, eh? Right, Frank? Not someone who wouldn't.'

'Listen Katie don't you start trying to soften me up.'

'You ask someone you think will come across, number one. Number two, they're the ones who are going to be a bit anxious, insecure, right Frank?'

'They might be . . .'

'So they're the ones . . .'

'. . . might be *kind*?'

'. . . they're the kind — what?'

'Might be the kind'll share a smoke?'

'Might be, Frank. But might be the kind'll be anxious about what . . .'

'Might be both.'

Kate's turn for silence.

'Might be kind *and* anxious, Kate!'

'What the hell are you two rabbitting on about?' B.J. has begun furiously to remove her clothes. 'You know, think I don't know what they like?' Her strong, ruddy body flings clear of T-shirt and pants. 'Think I haven't, you know, been told often enough?' She mimes the iron-pumping — her large breasts rise in muscular response. She turns to present them her smooth back, heavily dimpled waist above the emphatic cleft of buttocks,

109

straight legs and steady feet. 'Go on, Kate!'

'Go on what?'

'Go *on*!' And B.J. moves to tug Kate's sweatshirt above her lean ribs. Soon she's standing naked also — more angular, long legs — clavicles, ribs, wrist-bones — belly that a child has left with loosened striations, big black pubic bush.

'Frank?' B.J. staring at him where he's backed against the freezer.

'*Are you two nuts?*'

'Come on, Frank. You know, all's fair.'

With shaking hands, Frank removes his jeans and the black T-shirt with a Motorhead transfer. In skants, his skinny, immature body stoops in the dim room like a pale, unlit candle.

'Aw, come on, Frank,' says grinning Kate.

He steps out of the skants. His genitals dangle, disproportion-ately large between skinny legs. 'Now what?' His penis begins to twitch upright. Outside, they can hear the scramble of the bull-terrier's claws on the worn planks of the middleweight's porch.

'This.'

'*This?*'

It doesn't take long. His voluminous ejaculation splashes against Kate's attendant arm. B.J. holds his quaking head against her breasts.

'Know what B.J. stands for, Frankie?', gripping his skinny, trembling body. 'When I was a kid they used to, you know, call me Baby Jane!'

'What's,' Frank's muffled voice, 'that got to do with . . . ?'

'Wasn't that I didn't, you know, like them. I just . . .'

'. . . what's that got to do with . . . ?' struggling free. 'Why'd you do . . . ?'

'. . . I just didn't care! "Baby Jane"!'

'. . . why'd you do that to me, B.J.?'

'Why'd you let me, Frank?'

Frank stares — not so quick this time.

'"Baby Jane"!' B.J.'s triumphant laughter.

'Kate, why'd she . . . ?'

'"Do it do it with Baby Jane, again and again and again and again" . . .'

'Kate?'

'You know, that's what they used to sing!'

'*Kate?*'

'Only I never, you know, screwed them. Just,' B.J. mimes the middleweight's iron-pumping.

'What Baby Jane's saying, Frank,' Kate's humorous face tilts up at the window where reflected afternoon light enters in a dusty shaft, 'is that she knows what good boys like.'

'When they finally, you know, got to me,' chortles B.J., 'it was like having all those pathetic stalks prodding me — all the ones I'd seen give up the moment I grabbed them, so *easy!*'

'So why'd you have to go an' . . .'

'Oh, you know, I don't mind helping you out, Frank. We're . . .'

'. . . go and do that to . . . ?'

'. . . we're, you know, friends!' B.J.'s shoulders shake with laughter.

'. . . do that to me — *what?*' yells Frank. '*Friends?* An' you treat me just like, treat me like a fuckin' *dog?*'

From next door comes the thump of music. The woman's voice can be heard singing along. The athlete's joins in — a theatrical tremulous baritone. The words are indistinguishable but familiar.

'Hear that? Why'd you want to wreck that for them?'

'They're just lucky.' Kate's tone implies a quotation. 'Luck's not the same as justice.' It sounds like B.J., not Kate.

'If I was a *athlete*,' Frank staring at her as though noticing her nakedness for the first time, 'in the first place I mightn't believe you'd do anything with the stuff once you'd got it, and in the second place I mightn't care!'

'Aha, but!' triumphs B.J. 'They don't, you know, trust *us*. That means they'd believe us. Because they'd be afraid.'

'And that means you might do something with the stuff.' Frank's still looking at Kate. Key words — Geek training.

'It means they'd *believe* it.'

111

'Then why,' staring at Kate but talking to heavy-breathing B.J., 'bother with the freezer otherwise?'

'Very good, Frank,' quiet Kate, staring back at him.

'Because, Frank,' B.J.'s contralto rises toward song, 'if you have a gun, you don't have to use it, but it has to be known that you've "got one up the spout", you know, is that what they say? Otherwise, you haven't got a gun, you've just got a toy, you know, you're *playing*. Guns, we're not into, Frank. But if you've got a dick, Frank, you don't have to use it — but it has to be known you've got one up the spout, you know, otherwise it's only for playing with. Isn't that what they teach boys?' B.J.'s miming iron-pumping — the aroma of her heated body seems to fill the dusty room. Frank's giving her his Martian look — *What are ya*? 'You've got one, Frank, that you never use, but we just saw it had one, you know, up the spout. It's not a toy. They're not. And we've got a freezer we don't have to use, but it's not a toy, either.' Her loud peals of laughter have operatic qualities, a performer's confidence. 'You're a mutant, Frank. You're so bright, you know, if you had wheels you wouldn't just be a trolley, you'd invent an engine for yourself!' B.J.'s marvellous shoulders are shaking — she seems to stir dust across the room's shaft of sun.

But Frank crouches, quite still, staring at her.

'Full circle,' says Kate. 'Just like earlier, farting around after that red car. Back where we started. God almighty, B.J.'

'Trolley?' Frank's face now wears a lopsided grin. 'Ask me, I think you're all fuckin' mad.' He's begun to reassemble the freezer. 'Look at this!' He waves his skinny arm around the bare room. 'With no clothes on, talking about . . .'

But then he sees it pop into a different focus altogether — Kate's resigned, humorous silence, her long, tired body; B.J.'s operatic bliss, the anger that heats her strong limbs. When you're on the inside, it's possible — it's even real.

'Shit a brick.' He reaches for his clothes. 'You really *mean* it!' He puts the clothes down again. 'It's *we* — we're mad. *We're* all . . .' Like the pig-dog chasing its own aroma or itch, his expression circles around after meaning. When he stops, exhausted, he's still naked in a room with two naked women — one of them's just pulled him off, but it was never meant to be like this. It was meant to be the way he'd sometimes thought about it — dreamed about it: pinkish light, different furniture; not this dusty reflected glare of afternoon, this freezer. It was something he'd seen others doing — in heaps of bedding, in cars. He'd always been outside it: second-hand.

On the inside, it's different.

The scarred dog of his thought lies down.

From the other side of the wall comes the familiar but indecipherable sound of singing.

B.J.'s voice regains its no-nonsense timbre. 'You know, like I say, I think we need to talk this through. This whole "up the spout" thing. We need to do some work on it.'

22

THE MALE: THE DWARF OF LOVE — THE ENAMOURED SWAIN — THE pilgrim!

With ecstasy, Wallace perceives the speeding Valiant of the Chaffee Man swing into position behind her red streak.

At last it's coming out, the inside on the outside.

'Whip it out — whip it out!' Her cries join Jackson's.

'M24! Chaffee!' — beneath the plastic moustache, his teeth are bared in joy that resembles terror.

Finish with the going around in circles.

'Waddace! It's him!'

Why are they always afraid? That we'll eat them alive? Put them inside? Ha ha! The dwarf of love!

'It's him, Waddace!'

Slowing so as not to lose the Valiant at the town-hall lights, Wallace with one hand takes out her loaded one-shot Terumo and sees the stiff moustache fall from Jackson's nostrils as he squeezes down the plunger. His cries punch at the roof.

'What do you see, Jackson?'

'The sea, Wallace! Sunlight!'

So does Wallace. 'Anything else?'

'I see it all going along there and coming back here! It never stops, Wallace!'

'There's no end in sight . . .'

'I see glass, it's dark inside. Wallace, I see cake!'

Visionary. 'How's *he* doing?'

'Here he *comes*. Ooh wah, he comes, Wallace. He's *driving*! He's a dancer!'

Now you're talking. 'What else?'

'He's a gorilla, Wallace. Got hair on his face. He's a fighting man!' Jackson wears his yellow golf cap backwards so as to be able to face the rear without slowing the Porsche down. The back of his head looks forward as the red car's great tyres drum across railway tracks by the wharves. '*Them too*!'

'Them who? Who are you getting, Jackson, my boy?'

'In the old them womens with the blue at the other day when . . . they after *him*, Wallace! Mr Chaffee!'

Oh shit. 'The blue van?'

'Go, Mr Chaffee, go!'

'Jackson — "Mr Chaffee" is between us and them?'

'Yes, he is!'

'Try this, then: we are in front of both of them.'

'We are! We are!'

'Then they are both after us.'

' — '

'And police, Jackson. *They're* in front.'

From Samoa to the Marquesas, and then to the Society Islands. Then some to Easter Island. Some to Aotearoa, some to Hawaii. Some from the Marquesas straight to Aotearoa, some straight to Hawaii. It's a web, Wallace had told him — it all goes along here and comes back there; it never stops. It's history.

Look at you, Jackson: following a thread. Her fires had burnt away the screens on his vision, he could see himself on a dragline in the swarm. With fear he'd moved toward her bright venom. Navigated her boat along a coast she'd said was crawling with spiders — black iron-sand, a white line of breakers. 'In there, Jackson, above the tidemark. The red stripes. Dancing in the dunes!' Never could remember what she'd said. 'Shooting up katipo venom!' Eat fruit, swim, and fuck. 'You're a natural sailor, Jackson. Together we can bring the good news! That last crew — worse than useless, Jackson, I tell you. True north all the way. No instinct. So boring.'

'See them, Jackson?'

'Who? Wallace? Them spiders . . . ?' Jackson slumps under his brim.

'Open your . . .'

'. . . spiders with them stripes, them . . . ?'

'. . . open your eyes, Jackson baby, *look* — they've got stripes all right, but . . .'

'. . . them red ones, Wallace?'

'. . . but the wrong sort — *what*? Jackson, will you look? It's the *cops*.'

But Jackson's no longer communicating — beneath the yellow cap-brim his eyelids tremble upon a memory of white breakers along a coast of iron — the fiery navigation-aid, Wallace's pubic triangle — her voice that told him he was crawling on a web.

'Too much for you, huh, fella?' Beside her, Jackson lolls as though asleep. Too much stuff?

'Too much paradise?' shrieks Wallace as the Porsche tail-wags past the queue of cars at the motorway ramp, and past the oddly incurious faces of the traffic police there — dummy face-shields under visors — a manikin sheen on the skin — posed androids. 'Too much fucking carwash?' she yells at them. 'Too much tourist brochure!'

Perhaps Jackson's fainted.

In the rear-vision mirror she notes with satisfaction the battered Valiant hard a-heel — within she spies the swain, her pilgrim, her approaching dwarf.

No more going around in circles. This is the mating thread. Finished bouncing on the foundation threads. He's got his dragline in. It's tight. On to mating thread.

To origin and back. Right, left, left — is he trying to pass on the inside? Bouncing, bobbing, turning right and left, stretching and releasing.

She orients toward him.

Back there, as he draws alongside, she sees the blue van pull over, shepherded by a motorcycle cop.

She orients again. He's bouncing and bobbing, high intensity — stretching and releasing. Drumming with his legs. Dancing! She can see his mouth opening and shutting — a hairy face, cadaverous, black glasses — Mr Chaffee!

If only Jackson would wake up, we could decode this one.

Too soon for contact.

Spring apart.

Wallace presses her accelerator to the floor and feels the resisting earth surge beneath her backside. Let's see if this pilgrim means to risk everything. His gasping face has been left behind — his words that she won't hear until she's ready for a good acceptance posture.

The sea — sunlight. It's all going along here and coming back there. It never stops. It's dark inside. He's driving — Mr Chaffee!

Her nautical, pagan poet lolls beneath his yellow cap. Slowing so as not to seem to flee, she watches the Valiant persist along his thread: stretch, release — turn right, left, left — bobbing — down to contact — jump apart.

Oh he means it! He's a pilgrim! He's staying on the web, M24. With his black eyes and his mouth that could be shouting, or gasping for air, or singing — her dwarf swain!

Put him inside!

Within her, Wallace feels the inside swelling to be outside. This one I'll *eat*, she thinks. This one's for me.

She feels the hoards of dancing children pressing to be free.

Her pagan navigator dreams beneath his golf cap. Just more shark-tucker, scoffs Wallace.

But Mr Chaffee!

This one's not afraid.

23

IN THE PORSCHE THAT RED-HEAD PUTS HER FOOT DOWN, AND
Salvation goes cold all over at a memory of breakneck transport:
Route 13 out to the Meo resettlements at Ban Son, and any
Laotian taxi in open country was a suicide run. He'd sat sweating
on the plastic seat-cover of a Citroen that mixed smelly blue low-
octane smoke with its dust trail. Behind it, people clambered
back on to the road, out of the smoke. In the car, the priests
going up to visit the camps had told him matter-of-factly everything he needed to know about opium. They wore dark glasses
and smoked, and they had umbilicus wrist-thongs to make them
invisible. Salvation had often thought about the invisibility
charms later, after the leg.

Not now, though. Right now he was ringed with fire. He was
in lights. He was wired.

— Look at her *go*!

From the corner of his eye, Salvation sees two of those auction
mart grunts, the fat one and the old one, standing like idiots on
the footpath, and the wasted woman, skinny like a refugee Meo
at Ban Son. He leaves them behind in his rubber smoke. They
just don't feature.

Who does, right now? Not Sino-Viet Smokewalker Huu-you-
think the Smiler, but the poet To Huu maybe. Good name —
Who? — plenty of cover. Ha ha. The red Porsche seems to slow
for triumphantly laughing Salvation at the town-hall lights, and
he can see that the dark man in it is looking back at him, though
his yellow cap's turned arse-backwards.

> To be able to live, to die like you
> hating the enemy, loving your country;
> living, to be the bomb that explodes,
> dying, like the current of clear water.

118

To Huu wrote that for Pham Hong Thai in '56. In '24, Pham tried to assassinate Merlin, the Governor-General of French Indochina. The bomb didn't work. Pham leapt into the Pearl River.

It was the colours that were never real — the wet juicy pale greens of palms, humid air, saffron yellow cloth, orange marigolds littering the temples, black smoke like oil drifting in air, sky the colour of steam, blood jetting across flagstones.

They'd walk out of the smoke, so small they were like kids. Sometimes they *were* kids. They didn't feature and you left them behind. But even the press corps waiting for its whisperers in the Green Latrine in Vientiane came back round to them sooner or later. Either they were always there, walking out of it — or else you always came back to them.

Round and round in fucking circles. The Croix du Sud, Crock of Suds, in Saigon. Smiler Huu's warehouse across the Thai border by Aranyaprathet. Through the open verandah at Klaeng. Out of the corner of your eye. Always in the picture. Always stepping back into it, the kids. Back into the picture, back out of the smoke.

In his rear-vision mirror, Salvation spots the blue J4. Ahead, the Porsche veers at the motorway ramp and a police check-point. Round and around, like the armoured cavalry cloverleaf formation. And then you break out, you move ahead. In the red Porsche, the yellow cap has dropped from sight, but the red flag of hair, the woman's head, seems to flaunt across at the standing police.

Halt, deploy in circles, right flank, left flank, and ahead. Regroup, move out! Always circling back to the secure position. Then break out!

Maybe Salvation's the only one who now sees it's a beautiful day. He steers the awful pain in his leg down as though by an act like will into the howling motor of the Valiant. He can smell oil, he can smell the sea. He begins to close with the Porsche. It jigs close to the white lane-divider. Full on! Break out, encircle. He veers to outflank.

'To be able to live, to die like you' — it seems to be a song, a battle cry. Salvation's also yelling, 'Did you get . . . ?'

But once again, the Porsche arrows away — is she playing with him?

'. . . get my note?'

Now that sounds *pathetic*, growls Salvation, setting himself to tail the Porsche. All at once he doesn't much like the pain in his leg — he switches to the other one. How bland the glittering sea. *Did you get my note*, he scoffs. Track her, just track her. Stay there.

He also notes the absence of the blue van, of police, of smoke, of the Pearl River. There's nothing. Back in the pattern, back to base, back in the secure position.

The Porsche has again slowed. This time as Salvo moves out into the right-flank cloverleaf he leans across to wind the window down on the passenger side. He doesn't yell the lines of To Huu this time, nor the simpering *Did you get my* — he chokes — the sound of his tinny voice saying that, which had brought him back to base just as surely as the plucking forceps had those nights in Klaeng, birthplace of another poet, Santhorn Bhu. Can't remember a thing about the bugger, Salvation can't. Maybe never knew. Threw the out-of-date Papineau Guide away too soon. And everybody in Klaeng too busy trading Crater-maker Outsize.

It was no time for poetry.

'Hey! Want a tank?' screams Salvo as he draws level with the woman in the Porsche. *There* the colours were never real, but you were there. *Here* they're real, but you're not here. 'Wanna tank? M24 Chaffee? Hey, do you want to buy a tank? Hey? Hey!'

You'd wake up and see the stone stupas piercing mist, sky like turquoise steam, wet glare of early sun — it wasn't real and you knew where you were. 'Hey! Want to . . . ?'

The woman's face, a theatrical white, turns toward him, and Salvation is astonished to see her tongue flicker within her red mouth in blatantly erotic semaphore. Beside her, the man in the yellow peaked cap lolls mouth-open against the door.

'No,' steering dangerously close, 'a *tank*, you want a tank? Mitchell bomber cannon, twin Cadillac V8 . . . ?'

The Porsche begins to pull away as though drawn on an invisible wire.

'. . . concentric recoil, hydromatic transmission . . . ?'

She looks back once as Salvation leans across yelling, and her teeth show for a moment in a grin that leaves him gaping in her wake — pierced by an image so real he no longer knows where he is — jaw dropping the word *tank* into the silence in which he's drawn onward again into a circle, cloverleaf search technique that moves you ahead by bringing you back, always back, to where they're walking out of smoke and your last memory is of a wound like a grinning mouth — red, like one of the girls in the Green Latrine, but inside it a wobbling lascivious tongue of blood.

And the other image, that follows on-line and makes Salvation tramp his bad leg down again upon the turret's shaking pedal, is of armour pierced by 57 mm recoilless — an orifice with a fringe of impact-splatter, obscenely like bunker graffiti of something else entirely.

But now, however hard he presses his pain downward into breaking out, the red Porsche stays out of range. It leads him in what seems to be a circling manoeuvre around the foreshore of the glittering bay at whose far end the ludicrous toy city stands clear of mist or smoke, its cool towers reaching into blue sky, bleached out by distance, utterly real, nowhere.

Third Day

Third Day

24

MORNING OF THE THIRD DAY.

The water of the long bay so still it seems to heave with a single motion that makes Jackson feel sick. Behind the eastern ranges, dawn hurls a vivid parabola of salmony cloud across the washed-out blue sky. How can such calm be violent — this may not be the substance of what Jackson's thinking, but it's the form of what he fears.

Shoot up one load, it's better than carwash, it's like carwash all over your body — Jackson gloats and feels deathly all at the same time. Wallace never got it wrong before. One moment he felt the load tear into his brain, it was all going along here and coming back there.

And then next thing it was like jumping spiders jumping about jumping inside him. Dancing! — Jackson barely grins, and retches. And then when he woke up it was in a deck-chair facing east and that gorilla with the leg was coming on deck with Wallace — Jackson heard them, couldn't move a muscle, maybe it was the sound of the man's voice woke him up?

It was nearly dawn then. Jackson's eyelids peeling back off eyeballs that seemed smeared with sticky grey. A nodding sensation which he presently realised was the boat moored upon the darkness. Through a grey film he could see the outline of the hills in the east. Trying to move, he found himself unable to do so.

Dew, or sweat, running from his hair, his chin resting upon a wet blanket. And that gorilla's boots banging the deck as the light began to show out there.

We face the east! — voice like a pastor, but worn out, tinny, rattling.

He felt Wallace's hand on his cheek. He could smell her, potent and replete.

'We face the east! You, *mring kongvial*, spirit animal guardian.

125

You, *kruu*, spirit practitioner! *Ruup areak*, spirit medium!'

'Jesus fucking Christ,' Jackson heard Wallace mutter, as her warm palm carressed his chilly cheek. And then the hobbling clatter of the gorilla's boots along the jetty, a distant departing roar as he drove his Valiant away.

Jackson wanted to say *I can't move*, then, but he couldn't move his tongue or his jaw — couldn't raise his arms that hung down beside the deck-chair.

He sat watching the fluid surface of the planet buckle slowly, dangerous bolts of pink soar up from behind the hills.

I'm scared.

Wallace, I'm scared now.

I can't make any of me go.

Wallace it shouldn't be this quiet.

Wallace were we having fun?

And now as the red flags fade and the warmth of light smites him in the face (Jackson makes his eyes close) he smells Wallace back again — she's handpumped a shower and he can also smell coffee and bacon and hot bread and pawpaw — his body heaves again, it seems to fly open like a trap. Nothing comes out but a loud groan, but Jackson feels himself move — his knees hit the deck, and then he's on his feet grabbing at Wallace, missing, finding the deck-house to lean against.

'You all right, now, Jackson? Want some breakfast, fella?'

' — '

'Take your time,' says Wallace smoothly. 'Boy, have I got news for you.'

'Who, that, he . . . ?' Jackson's tongue lolls upon his lower jaw.

''s right. All the way, boy. I believe he'd have driven into Cook Strait if he'd thought it would get him to the end. A grade-A lunatic, Jackson. Just what the doctor ordered.'

Wallace crunches on a hot bacon sandwich, she lifts a steaming white cup to her face.

'Wallace, what . . . ?'

'You missed your stroke, Jackson. My God, and I thought you could *take* it. I mean, haven't I done enough work on you yet?'

126

Wallace scoops a curl of pawpaw into a spoon. 'Want some? *Fruit*, Jackson? No?' Facing the full early sunlight, Wallace slides the fruit on to her tongue. 'I'm only kidding, Jackson. What made you turn yourself off like that?'

'Wallace, what was it?' Jackson feels as though he's mixing concrete with his tongue.

'What was what?'

'That . . .' — with wobbling fingers, Jackson mimes plunging the one-shot Terumo.

'Oh, *that*!' Wallace's elaborate laughter has to find its way around her mouthful of food. 'That was to make you *dance*, Jackson!'

Jackson wants to say, But it didn't.

Then he feels some lines of information converge in his fearful thoughts.

'Wallace, was that . . . ?'

'Surely you're used to it by now, Jackson?'

'. . . was that, them spider, you know, along the coast when we, that you was always talkin' about — them, that *ki te po*? Wallace?' His whole face falls open with exhaustion.

'"Ki te po", Jackson? *Night*?'

'*Night*, Wallace?'

'Or, death?'

'*Death*?'

'*Te po*, Jackson. That's death — that's night.'

'Why, Wallace?' Jackson sinks to sit on the deck. Weeping is an effort he can hardly manage on top of everything else. 'You trying to, *kill* me, Wallace?'

'Good heavens, Jackson. What a bizarre hallucination.'

'But them *spiders*, Wallace!'

'But they're not night, Jackson. Not nasty ol' *death*, Jackson. They're the dawn! They're the red stripes! They're when you wake up and dance, Jackson!'

'*Ki te po*?'

'Katipo, Jackson. The katipo spider. *Latrodectus katipo*, Jackson — the female, of course. Oh dear, I can see where language has switched the tracks.'

But now Jackson is too tired to mix more words. His thoughts heave upon a queasy darkness, where he's been — and that sense of insect life swarming, dancing through his body. And then the red streaks of the dawn, Wallace's white white legs bent back upon the deck of her boat, devouring the breakfast he can see she'd thought was meant for him — and she's watching to see whether she's right about her feeling that he's not going to ask the question again.

You make me shoot a load of them spiders in, Wallace?

'*We face the east!*' Wallace snorts, miming Salvation's tinny voice, tipping more coffee from a thermos jug. 'My God, was that ever a lulu, Jackson.'

See? — she's not going to talk about it.

'Know what he wanted?'

I think he wanted you, Wallace.

'He wanted — wait for this, Jackson — he wanted to sell me, us, a *tank*!' Wallace squeals with laughter.

Mr Chaffee. Crazylegs. You the sunrise, Wallace. You the . . .

'A tank! Jackson? Doesn't that . . .'

. . . you the sunset too.

'. . . strike you as outrageous? Jackson? Know what . . .'

You the dawn. You the dark night. *Te po.*

'. . . a M24 Chaffee, actually *is*, Jackson? Guess.'

We done it, Wallace. We done it in the carwash. M24, Wallace. Chaffee!

'Good grief, Jackson, you're making me nervous. You look like an Easter Island statue, for God's sake. Nod if you can hear me, Jackson? If you're functional?'

Jackson tries to shake his head — No, can't hear you, Wallace. Can't hear you talk about that Mr Chaffee. But it seems his head will fall off and roll into the harbour.

'It's a tank, Jackson. With a gun. You know what I'm talking about?'

No, Wallace. Can't hear you.

'He says he brought it back in bits from South-East Asia. You should see his leg, Jackson. Somebody must've tried to blow it off. He's really unreal, pardon me. And then . . .'

128

Remember what you said, right at the beginning, Wallace —
Can you drive a boat, I jus' lost my entire crew?

'. . . then he started on about children — *smokewalkers*, he
called them. And get this: some Vietnamese mastermind called
Than Giong, the child who wakes to lend its heart to the iron
horse of liberation, Jackson! Got that? And the guy isn't even a
poet like you, Jackson.'

Sure, lady, I said. So I drove your boat, Wallace — washed
your car, too, ha ha. Had plenty of fun. You saw I remembered
everything. So, Wallace — Wallace, why I started . . .

'And then he's telling me all this stuff about Cambodian, about
Khmer sorcery, about animal spirits, spirit guardians, Jackson?
Get it? We're absolutely double-tracking, Jackson, him and us,
but I swear, I never so much as . . .'

. . . why I started getting scared, Wallace? All the time? After
you started giving me stuff, down along that spider coast,
Wallace?

'. . . I never breathed a word about spiders to him, Jackson, I
swear, and he . . .'

Was it *spiders* you was giving me, Wallace?

'. . . he just immediately saw that I had this animal spirit
guardian connection? Isn't that unbelievable? Jackson?'

Was it?

'Didn't I tell you they'd find us? All you had to do was stay
tuned?'

Jackson switches back to her. He can see her mouth working
away — can't tell if it's on breakfast or words. Beyond her, the
lone fisherman has taken up his daily station. Early traffic has
begun to pass. Jackson can see the Porsche parked as usual at the
edge of the marina. He spots his yellow golf cap on the jetty.

'Jackson? You get any of that? Do you read me?' She's snap-
ping her fingers.

All he can remember, is a white line of surf drawn between
himself and beaches of black iron-sand — Wallace's red pubic
delta in the bows. That, and waking upon darkness that shifted
beneath him, red streaks of light.

'Jackson? You begin to disappoint me.'

The lone fisherman makes his single cast of the day and settles back to watch what seems to be a clumsy grappling dance performed upon the rocking deck of the big motor launch. They're up early. The red-haired woman's shriek comes just before the splash. Just after the splash comes the sound of the big Island joker's loud laughter — 'Drown, ya bitch!'

Some people have all the fun.

25

A BARE FLOOR, A TELEVISION, THREE BEANBAGS, THE FREEZER —
vague light comes through the dusty window and falls upon
B.J.'s sullen discussion group.

Or, as Frank quips, 'What comes out of the taps.' Everyone
gets a 'turn'. 'So to speak.' Quick as a flash, Frank. 'Sure you
don't want to do it in the bath, B.J.? With snorkels on?'

Kate: 'Okay — *I'll* start.'

'One day I won't forget in a hurry, was when Janie took off
with her father in the plane for Aussie. She had this flight bag
with a doll in it, only the doll couldn't fit, one of its legs was
sticking out. The quack had me on all this dope, I could hardly
talk. I remember trying to say to Janie, your bag's like my heart,
I can't get all of you in it, you're too much to fit. And then she
pottered off happily to the bloody plane with that pink leg
sticking out of the bag, it was a big adventure. I didn't see her
for a long time.'

'Couple of years. And then I went over. First thing I said,
when I got the chance, was, remember the doll you couldn't get
in your bag? Because it was what *I'd* remembered. Poor bloody
kid, she went all shy, she remembered all right, it was the thing
that went on reminding her of her mad mother. Dave told me
she'd asked for a new doll, a small one. When he asked why, she
said something like it was so she could fit and the zipper would
work. He had to get rid of the old one, the big one, because the
kid wanted to stay small and didn't want to be reminded of me,
or something. How about *that*.'

'Nearly twenty. She didn't stay small. She's long, like me, got
these legs like a racehorse, big mouth full of teeth, really lovely
hands . . .'

131

'. . . and one day — belt up, Frank — she's going to be insuring them for a bloody fortune, I can tell you.'

'She's a musician. She plays the cello, would you believe? Benefits of a rich bloody father. But she's good. Last time I saw her, I said play something for me, something just for me, the right piece. She didn't even hesitate. She just closed her eyes and played a Bach unaccompanied suite, Suite 5 in C minor, I damn near know it by heart. I was looking at the way her feet turned out on the wooden floor, every so often her big long toes would all bunch up, especially during the *sarabande*. Dead corny, eh. She started crying from the very start — so did I — but she kept her eyes shut mostly, the tears just squeezed out and ran down her face. At the end she opened her eyes, all red, and gave me this amazing bloody smile, her nose was running too, all over the place, she just sat there dripping with her feet turned out on the trendy wooden floor and said, Isn't that beautiful? I said it was the saddest bloody music I'd ever heard. That's right, she said — isn't it beautiful? That's what I always play for you, when I think of you. It knocked me out, I can tell you. She's still too much for me — I can't fit her in. She's bloody fantastic.'

'Of *course* I miss her! And she does love me, in a way. But the, her stepmother, the woman Dave married's been good to her, she's got three half brothers and a little sister, an accident, Dave's a big bloody academic with piles of dough, she's been to Europe a few times, she'll probably go there to study music, they all had a year at some bigwig university in the States a while back, he's into genetic engineering or some such, how can *I* compete? Dave even keeps a flat in bloody London, that he shares with a couple of other academic bigwigs, Janie'll probably stay in it if she studies in London. Or maybe she'll go to New York. Jesus. I'm just her crazy bloody mother that ran away with some hippie lunatic years ago that everybody says went and drowned himself . . .'

'Yes, she *does* know, B.J., these days that's not much for her to handle, she's even kind of proud in a way. Certainly beats the other image, me in bloody clapped-out vans with yin-yang signs on. First time the subject came up, was the trip when she played me that Bach, she was seventeen then. She asked me if I was living with anyone these days. I said I was living with a woman called B.J. Don't you have anything to do with men, she said. I said not any more. She said, are you a lesbian? I said, I suppose you could say that — after a while men just didn't do anything for me any more, in fact they annoyed me most of the time, they made me want to get out of the way of their boozy breath. And the nice fellows bored me — I hated them being understanding when they didn't understand bloody *shit*. Maybe I didn't put it quite like that. She gave me another of those over-the-top smiles. I know what you mean, she said. They expect you to be impressed. They expect you to like whatever they do, they don't even take the trouble to find out what's nice. Why, I said, do you, have you, are you, blah blah — Christ, what did I bloody expect, her mother, wasn't even around when she had her first period. Of course, she said, but don't worry, only a couple, it's no fun unless *I* decide. I won't get caught napping like *you*, Mum! Most of the time I'd sooner have the cello between my legs. Hey — not bad, eh? My daughter! But she doesn't make me feel like an idiot. She's not ashamed of me or anything. I don't embarrass her. But somewhere way back along the line, was that thing about the bloody doll. I mean, she traded it for another one, one that wouldn't stick out. Know what I mean? She kind of tidied up. I don't know how much she knew. But there was something going on in there, all those years. She sorted it out, she had to. I suppose when I heard that music for the first time I got a shock — I thought, she's run something beautiful and something sad together and it's her way of remembering me, it's how she tucks that sticking-out bit in. It's how she makes room in her heart. I don't know, maybe I'm making it up. The way her toes bunched up while she played, I thought, oh my God what's going on in there? And the crying. But she played it so straight, nothing sloppy . . .'

'. . . no, not "kind of uptight" either, if you don't mind, Frank! She didn't hold back, I mean she had goo running out of her nose and she wouldn't stop playing to wipe it, she just kept licking it off her top lip, like a little kid. But she played really straight, she was *listening*, it was with her mind as well as her heart. I think she's okay, she's strong. She doesn't put me down and she doesn't blame me . . .'

'. . . oh, well, he was *always* too bloody good to be true, B.J. Lucky for him that woman he went away with and then married had a stack of bloody kids, otherwise he'd probably have thought he knew it all. Ah, he's all right. He's kind, he's been excellent to his kids, to Janie, he's a liberal — you know, you know what I bloody mean. He's *understanding*, he probably pulls that understanding thing with the good-looking young students he screws, bet on it.'

'Bitter and twisted, Frank? Maybe I bloody am a bit. I know his type, Frank, you don't. I'll bet he's into feminism. He's got a bloody exercycle in the basement, he's quite up to date with the kids' stuff, he has discussions with them about it all, the music, the sport, politics, movies, you know. He's *good*. He's professional. He's professionally good. That's how I know he screws his bloody students. Men can't be that good without unloading *somewhere*! If he was a television farmer with a little bloody house on the prairie somewhere, he'd have a fucking favourite *pig* or something stashed away in the barn. That way he can come back on screen with his smile intact and help with the washing-up. You can't smell pig on TV. But I used to smell the formaldehyde on Dave. Maybe he was into, maybe he was a necrophiliac! That would account for the super smile!'

'I know, Frank, I know . . . did I say frogs? A frog-fucker — a *dead*-frog-fucker! Excuse me, I really do have a high regard for the creep, but I have to get a laugh in now and then. It used to drive me crazy thinking of him bringing up Janie. Can't tell you what I used to imagine. Of course, I had an ally, that was his *next* wife, she made sure he remembered the smell of baby poo. She's pretty good. I used to think she was a bloody little slut. Of course, he pulled the understanding bit on her all those years ago, only then it was in reverse — she had to be understanding about *his* life with this neurotic bloody woman, whom he'd married because she was bloody pregnant, you know, it was the story of our lives back then in the sixties.'

'Jane? She likes her stepmother. They have this joke, because Hannah, that's, you know, her — because Hannah was a biology student as well back then, she and Janie have this joke: What, *Hannah* give up biology? Nah, just shifted from Pure to Applied. Because, you know, Hannah was, she's pretty bright, too. Oh well, you get the picture. She's okay. But she's not going to play second fiddle to the Professor, no way. They get on pretty well. She doesn't squeeze him, he doesn't leave her out of the conversation. I can't bloody stand it. And Janie knows he wasn't cut out for a life with me. I mean, I don't go over there every few years and gossip about her father. But I've told her that he used to find me a bit overpowering — I used to make demands, know what I mean? I was a bit bloody ripe for him. He was always a bit fastidious. Anyway, I told her this because I thought she ought to know the truth about power and fathers and stuff — shit, mothers and daughters used to be allowed to discuss these things, it's only the few generations before us that put pants on table legs, all that. I wanted to tell her, anyway. She'd played that music for me, didn't even hesitate, she had it right there in the front of her head, in her heart, she'd been talking to me with that, I had a lot of ground to make up. So I told her that her father'd found me a bit too much — in all sorts of other ways, too. I mean, that was probably how she got conceived, I didn't give the poor twerp time to be sensible. Too impulsive.'

'Oh, ha, ha, Frank. How droll.'

'Okay, okay, we can hear you, no need to flog it to death. Mind if I go on? The point was, he was, he just wasn't in my class, all right? Frank? Anyway, she loves him, her father. That's normal. And she knows she's always been a bit special for him. So I thought, maybe she'll think I'm putting him down — a ball-breaker, like they say. So I said, Do you think I'm a ball-breaker, you know, whatever? But she was quite upset. Oh no, she said. I think lots of boys *are* a bit scared. That's what makes them angry. Dad's just kind of transitional.'

'*Transitional*, Frank! And then she said, And he knows it — he's acting it out. He's being good. Not bad, eh? No bloody flies on Janie. Not just some over-protected smartarse, either. I wish it was me who'd brought her up, oh God. I wish I'd had that. I even wish I could take the credit for her being perfect, such a perfect . . . and I miss her, I miss her a hell of a lot, sometimes . . . ah, shit, that's it — someone else have a go.'

'Well, I can't hardly even remember my mum or my dad. I can remember Dad catching the bus. That was the last time I seen him. It was a fuckin' Railways bus, it went from platform nine. All I can remember is, he bought a paper at the station shop, and give me a packet of Smarties. His back going up the steps into the bus. There was lots of people catching a train for Auckland at the same time as the bus was going wherever it was — I never knowed where he was going. I was more interested in the train. There was little kids like me all over the show, they all had pillows. Mum give me a smack because I kept on about the pillows, and then we took off. Taxi to Lyall Bay. Mum was sharing a flat there with one of Geek's sisters. She was miles older, the sister. We used to call her Auntie Peg. She worked for Geek at something or other, maybe she used to mind his scungy little shop while he went out looking for all the shit he put in it.'

'Nah — what I remember best of all is all the junk in the shop. After I went to school, I used to go there after because Mum was working. I used to play there. That sister, Auntie Peg, she'd gone. We had the same flat. The stuffing gradually come out of the sofa — I used to haul chunks out. But Geek never give us a new one, though he used to have untold in the shop. But it was a neat place to play. He had old furniture, and then these bargain bins of real junk, like nuts and bolts and shit, and old Army surplus stuff, and old hats and shoes, all kinds of clapped-out appliances, it was cool. And then one day after I'd been at fuckin' school about a year, Mum didn't come to collect me from the shop after school, I mean after work. Fuckin' old Geek come in, and seen me, he says aren't you home yet — where is the bitch? Or something like that. Mum had a machinist job somewhere in town, all I knew was that it was through the tunnel from Hataitai. I used to like going through the tunnel on the bus when Mum took me to town sometimes. Mostly I played at Lyall Bay. And at Geek's. At Geek's I used to play by myself, Geek wouldn't let other kids in. But in the holidays all us kids used to fart around on the beach, the swings by the surf club, all that. Where is the silly bitch, he said. That was the last I heard of her. No one ever said anything. I went back to Geek's place that night, we had fish and chips for tea, I watched TV and went to sleep in a chair, and that's the way it was for quite a few months — Geek used to drop me off for school about a hour earlier than anyone else, I used to have money for a pie, after school I come to the shop and played, for tea we usually had some takeaways, I used to go to sleep in a chair. After about a year Geek fixed up a room for me and I had a fuckin' bed and all that. I used to dress in stuff from the shop. Sometimes he'd bring soccer boots or something, but I soon sussed this was going to be one of his bright ideas — like, tramping boots meant I'd be off into the wet fuckin' bush for a few weeks in the holidays. Once he come home and slung a wetsuit into my room, it'd come in to the shop, but it was too big, I never found out what he had in mind — fuckin' *salvage* prob'ly, ha ha.'

'No, Kate — never heard from her again, Kate. Can't really remember asking Uncle Geek either, you know, When's Mum coming to pick me up, Uncle Geek? Used to fall asleep in the chair before I got the chance, anyway I liked it at Geek's, and old Geek was always farting about with all his junk, sometimes the house used to be stuffed with it. And then when he started getting me involved in all them activities, it was like his idea of bringing me up, *he* didn't have the time was what he was always saying — didn't have the time to cook tea at night, or he'd open tins . . .'

'No way, B.J., there was never any sign of a woman on the scene, probably if I hadn't been camping there he wouldn't even come home sometimes, sometimes used to drop me off with enough for pizza or whatever and bugger off again himself, Got to take some deliveries, was what he was always on about, he was into all kinds of bent stuff, bet on it. Couldn't have no little talking head looking on, could he?'

'What? Well, he *did* fuckin' like me, in a way, Kate. No one else did. During that soccer phase Geek used to catch the last parts of the games, used to stand there on the sideline with all the mums and dads and scream blue murder! Then we'd get a hamburger in Kilbirnie and he'd drop me off. That was Saturdays. I used to do the washing on Saturdays too. That was my job. I used to bung the whole fuckin' lot in one of them flip-flops and let it thrash away all afternoon. My soccer gear with mud, the sheets, my clothes, Geek's heap from his bedroom floor, the fuckin' lot. It all come from the shop anyway, when it wore out you just grabbed another pants or whatever. Then there was the sea cadets phase, that was a bloody dag, you was meant to have all this kind of flash Navy gear? — well, it didn't survive the washing-machine I can tell you! Thrashed the arse off it in about two fuckin' tries. And what is the meaning of this, said that lieutenant prick — what's the meaning of this, *my lad*? What a turd. It must have been around then that I asked about my mum and dad — kind of like a formal enquiry, you know? It was around the sea cadet time. Don't know where your old man went to, says Geek, but I should think it was a long way from your mother. And where's she, Uncle Geek? Dunno, son, but I'll bet it's a long way from you.'

'Yeah, that was that, Kate. That was something like how it went. Old Geek could make you laugh. Old Geek was okay. He was right in a way. By the time I got to high school I was streets ahead. I knew a hell of a lot. I could fix things, I could get into things, and I could get out of things, too, if you know what I mean — but it was all like junk, it was chuck-out just like me, it was all stuff that someone else was finished with, everyone else but Geek. Even that computer class — like, I got brought up in a fuckin' junk shop, I could tell the difference, I could tell that the teacher was just pulling down fuckin' *income*. And then he tried me on. Hand in the pocket. Fuck that. That was when I shot through — no more junk, no more bright ideas of Uncle Geek's.'

'You must be joking, B.J. — I didn't need a fuckin' job. Did you guys, sorry, did youse advertise for a *handyman* or something? I always just found it. It found me. And I was down at Social Welfare, you're mad not to get on the dole, how can they stuff you into some awful fuckin' job when there aren't any and the ones there are take one look at you and send you back.'

'Well, okay B.J., when you saw me things had slipped a bit. Got chucked out of a house. Had a bit of a, the cops come round for a talk, you know, they didn't have nothing on me but they was close. So I was in this Railways hut at the Thorndon yards. And then one day at fuckin' Social Welfare there you was with the van, jammed starter. Simple. Nothing to it.'

'Nah, Kate, I meant nothing to my fuckin' *life*, you know, what a non-event. No cellos and shit, ha ha. Sorry, Kate. No offence. Just a joke. Away you go, B.J.'

'Well, you know, God, you surprise me, Kate!'

'Yes, I have kept quiet till now, and no, Kate, I couldn't give a damn about what you've told me and what you haven't, you know, before now — I mean, there's plenty you don't know about *me*, right? I mean, you know, we all need space for our

139

own creativity, for dreaming, for self real' . . .'

'I am *not* brooding, Kate! God!'

'No, Kate, it was that, you know — what was it you said just now? — that "I suppose you could say that" when your, you know, when Jane asked if you were . . .'

'No, this is *not* "another lecture"!'

'What do you mean, Kate, "never miss a chance"!' I know we agreed, you know, to take turns . . .'

'Yes, it *was* my idea. But . . .'

'I know, I know — but "I suppose you could say that", you know, Jesus, Kate! I mean, you know, that's the point! How can you pass on such a, you know, such a feeble, such an unassertive . . . how could you come on like that to your own *daughter*!'

'I know I haven't got any! What are you trying to say, Kate — that I don't, you know, have an attitude? You know, that you have to be raped before you can have an attitude to it? Have to . . . ?'

'*My* mother? Kate? All right, you know, let's talk about *my* mother. She spent her entire life saying "I suppose" and "sort of" and "maybe" and "um", Kate. Doing what she was told, that's what! You know, when to cook, when to clean, when to spend money, when to get the kids to bed, when to lie down on her back! When my father died she didn't know *anything* — how to open a bank account, you know, take out insurance, pay tax. She couldn't even pick up the phone to ask someone! Too worried about being, you know, a nuisance. Probably worried about seeming stupid, too. It was like she'd spent her whole grown-up life in a locked ward or something, you know, like all those stories about people who were kept from the world or raised by

140

wolves or something, you know, and when they come out they are like innocents? Well, the locked ward was my father's life, my mother just lived completely inside that. Everything my father did kept her from knowing what happened outside. And inside was this really intelligent woman, you know, as well as being what they all call a devoted wife and mother she was really intelligent, only she put it all into her children — what?'

'*It shows*, Frank? Frank, are you trying to . . . ? Okay, Frank, you know, last fucking chance, I'm serious. But — *what*?'

'*Lucky*, Frank? Me?'

'What do you mean, you? *You* lucky? Listen, dickhead, I listened to you, you know, to your tale of woe, all right?'

'All right. But, what I was saying, but she didn't have any left for herself. And what I want to tell you — what gave it away was the way she told us stories. She had this way of hesitating, or pretending to, as though she couldn't work out what had to happen next. So, you know, we had to help her out, us kids, we had to decide! It wasn't, you know, that kind of *leading* kids, feeding them lines, you know. But it was like she'd offer a kind of choice, and whatever we chose she'd, you know, go on from. And then the story would get told again and again, and always the same decisions would happen, we'd get to know them.'

'Three brothers, a sister. Two older brothers, older sister, younger brother. So it was mostly me and my kid brother, right, Frank? He was an accident, like they say, ha ha, meaning Mum was probably too tired to remember.'

'Yeah, I'm getting to that, Kate. There *was* one special story. After it we seemed to get more into books. I always knew it was about, you know, something else, this story. Mum told it over and over. The last time she changed the ending. It was such a shock, you know, we just sat there, me and John, and she walked out of the bedroom and left the light on. Then Dad came in and turned it off. He usually came in after it was off and gave us one of those kiss-and-a-pat numbers, you know, like Go to sleep now my darlings, like, really, you know, *Shut up*. Only this time we were still sitting up, we'd just heard this weird ending to the story, Mum walked out fast and maybe she was crying, and then Dad came in and turned the light off — Good night, boom, you know, just like that, shut the door! We didn't have the foggiest, of course. We sat there bawling, but quietly. What I remember best is the feeling that, how do say it? — you know, it was like a kid's version of someone messing up the order of the universe, like that science fiction line "That morning the sun rose in the west", you know?'

'All right, all right, Frank, hold your horses — but let me tell you about how I remember the ending first, you know, because that night I literally turned my bed around, I slept with my head at the other end. Maybe it was so I could watch the door, but I think it was also because, you know, Mum had turned the world around that night — I had to get lined up with it? I can remember the feeling of tucking in the pillow end and pulling out the other one, and trucking down there with my pillow, John bawling away on the bottom bunk, What are you doing, what are you doing, why are you doing that for? It felt like, you know, the right thing to do, I can remember that. It feels as though I can remember that. Next morning Mum made the bunk up same as usual but I changed it round again that night, and so on — it went on like that for, you know, months. Okay, the story. Once upon a time there was a ginormous eel.
On the bank there was a windmill that sucked the river up to a tap in a house.
At night the moon used to sail right down the narrow sky above the dark gorge.
There would be the windmill's tin vanes flicking around in the moonlight.
There would be the ginormous eel listening to his river getting sucked away into a tap.

142

In the house there lived a woman. She was very good at singing. What she liked best were songs about sailing ships. (We usually sang a few here, and "Row Row Row Your Boat" and stuff.) But the sea was a long way from the river and the windmill. It was where the moon went after sailing along the narrow sky above the dark gorge and the ginormous eel.

It was where the sun went, too, but you couldn't look at it otherwise all you'd ever see afterwards would be like the flicking of the windmill's tin vanes in the moonlight. You wouldn't ever be able to see the big tomato sauce neon in Newmarket!

This was what the eel looked at. Not the neon. He didn't like tomato sauce. He liked soy sauce. And miso. He'd been to Japan. He was scared of sushi, though. Where was I?

Oh yes — he looked at the tin vanes in the moonlight. He thought, Hmmm. When the sun came up, he went to sleep.

But at night he looked at the tin vanes flicking in the moonlight, he listened to his river being sucked up to a tap in a house, he listened to it running into a bath, he listened to the woman singing songs about the sea. Oooo-eee.

The eel knew about the sea. He'd been to Japan and back. But the river was what he liked best.

It came from the cool stony mountains where there weren't any taps. The closer to the sea you got, the more taps there were. The more drains, too. The more paint factories. Ugh.

Maybe the woman singing in her bath, singing about sailing ships, didn't know about oil tankers.

In her dream, the moon was flickering like on the tin windmill vanes, on the sails of ships on the ocean.

One night the moon seemed to hang still above the dark narrow gorge. The windmill was slowing it down.

It was time to act.

The ginormous eel entered the pipe and was taken up to the tap. In her bath the woman lay.

Who knows, perhaps the creaking of the windmill reminded her of the creaking of sailing ships. Creee-eak. Spooky.

Okay.

(Mum wouldn't have said that. She'd have said Well now.)

Well now.

How — do — you — think — she — felt — when — a — voice — spoke — to — her — from — the — tap!

I am the eel of the dark gorge.

What do you want.

I want to come out of the tap.

I won't let you. Eeee!

I want to swallow you up!

I won't let you!

(We used to do these bits like a chorus. John and me.)

I won't let you!

I want to take you to the ocean!

I won't let you!

I want to show you oil tankers.

I don't want to see them!

Paint factories.

Yuk!

Your windmill is ugly.

I love it. Its flickering vanes, its clank.

I want you to look at the sun on the ocean.

I love the moonlight on the river.

I want to gobble you up!

No. Help!

I want to come out!

NO!

See this muscle of water coming out of the tap?

Yes.

It's me! See the shadow, the moonshine?

Yes.

It's me too. Here I come!

'Neat, eh! — what?'

'You bet it was, scary, Kate! That — what?'

'Making it up, Frank? You . . . ?'

144

'Wait on, let's get this straight. You know, you don't believe my . . .'

'Shut up, is this right? — you don't believe my mother'd . . . '

'Okay, all right, never mind. Just testing eh, Frank? You know, I'm sorry for you too, Frank, you know, shit! But, anyway, you bet it was scary! That was, you know, the fun of it. We used to play it in the bath, too.'

'Oh, very funny, Frank, he's really sparking, shit.'

'Not unless, you know — not unless he pipes down — what?'

'*Pipes*, eh Frank? You know, with a sense of humour like . . .'

'. . . a sense of humour like yours, Frank, you — four? Four what?'

'Four times this month?'

'Only if this little shit, you know — only if he . . . okay. In bed, that *Here I come*, Mum used to pull the covers up over our heads. We'd take turns getting eaten up by the dark. There were lots of versions. Sometimes, you know, she'd add like these satellite stories to it. But the basic stuff was always the same — you know, the eel, the dark, the moon, the windmill, the woman, the bath, the sailing ships, getting eaten up. People she'd read about in the newspaper used to live along the bank, you know, and people we knew — she used to embellish it with real stuff. Like the tomato sauce neon. Then, you know, it was dark and she'd turn the light out. It's funny, you know, but I can remember lying there and I nearly always had this picture in my head of the sea with moonlight. What do you call it, negative, you know, negative suggestion? She, Mum, took the dark away with the story. Shit. Lend us your hanky, Kate?'

'Thanks. What — the *other* ending? Can't you guess?'

'Look, don't even think about it Frank, really. I'm . . .'

'Okay. Well, it was more or less like this. I am the eel of the dark gorge.
I know.
I want to come out of the tap.
Come out.
I want to swallow you up.
Good. Do it. *Do it*. And then she ran out crying and left the light *on*. You know. Oh *Jesus* I can remember how it felt. And then suddenly it was dark and Dad slammed the door on us. And the next step was, you know, this is easy — the next step was Do it do it with Baby Jane again and again and again and again. Yeah, that shut you up, didn't it Frank! Didn't it just! The thing I loved was, you know, feeling them go soft. One after the other. I could make them. Sometimes there'd be three or four standing around wanking while they watched me do one. Lunch hour, after school, didn't matter. It was like remote control. You know, it was like turning on taps, that's dead right! You should see yourself, Frank! Funny now, but oh, then it was pure power!'

'No, it doesn't *turn me on* now either, Frank, I'm running out of patience with you. Sorry Frank, I just can't, you know, get close to taps. Ha ha.'

'Oh yes, I did love my father, Kate. But he was just so reliable. He was just so in control. Nothing I did could matter, know what I mean? You know? Because he would just approve of it, you know?'

'No I did *not*. Cut it out, Frank.'

'Yeah, okay, *seriously* I know it happens. Don't we all. But I'll tell you something, Frank, you know, for free — authority and cocks, power and cocks, it's one and the same. You can always

146

turn off a tap. I knew that was true of Dad too. Men with confidence, competent men, arrogant men — they're always been the ones I wanted to turn off most. Make them soft.'

'Do I have to spell it out, Frank? Make my father soft. Soften him. But then, I'm like Katie — I can't stand yes-men either. No-win situation, you know. When they're soft, you despise them. When they're hard, you know, you want to make them soft. Who cares. It's one way.'

'My mother, sing? Why do you want to know that, Kate?'

'Well, if *you* don't know why you want to know, I can't tell you.'

'You just want to know. Well, Kate — as a matter of fact, she couldn't. But Dad used to sing all the time — it was him, you know, who used to sing sailors' songs and shanties and things in the bath. That's probably how it got into Mum's story. Sometimes he used to sing in the car, when we went on holiday. But he always had to go back to the office early.'

'*What?* Oh, yeah, well Mum said, after he died, she told me he was always into some other woman, not that she put it like that. Or she said she always thought he was. Bet he was.'

'Well, one thing I remember. From . . .'

'. . . from when, do you mind, Frank? From when I was a kid. They, you know, my parents, used to have these cocktail parties. Me and the older kids, we used to hand round plates, the grownups'd make a fuss of us. My father used to call me, he called me Popsie, you know . . .'

'Popsie. You know, he'd say, "You're the prettiest girl in the room, as far as I'm concerned they can ship the rest back." Once I caught him and this woman on the porch outside the kitchen, she was wiping his mouth with a napkin, you know. He said something to me about the damned sauce. They both went off into fits, you know, laughing. My father's laugh . . . When I told Mum a lady'd wiped sauce off Dad, wasn't that nice of her, and funny, you know, I expected her to laugh as well. I didn't know why it was funny, but I knew it was a joke. I couldn't work out why she, you know, why she didn't laugh, as well. I thought I must've got it wrong. Later, you know, I . . .'

'*Die of*, Frank? Heart attack. Does it matter? In the office lift. They found him in the morning. He had a business dinner and went back to dictate notes into his machine. It was after the cleaners and all that. So they found him on the floor of the lift in the morning. The boss. The, you know, hard man. Stiff all right. You getting this, Frank? But dead, too. Turned off, you might say. Any questions?'

'It's all right, Frank, you fucking moron, Jesus, what a, come over here. I know you can't help it, Frank. It's all right. Shit, give us that hanky back? Thanks. You know . . . thanks.'

26

GLARING PALLID SKY THE COLOUR OF CONCRETE. THERE ARE buckets of canna lilies outside the hospital shop — they burst out like flames from buildings. Occasional heavy raindrops hit the hot pavement and evaporate, but a new spray of blood across the front steps of the hospital retains a sticky surface sheen.

The racket of traffic is cut off as the door shuts behind the skinny girl — walking in from the smoky miasma of exhaust fumes. Her head of bright short hair quests this way and that. Behind her, the very fat man bears an immense conflagration of canna lilies. His helpless smile tracks Snag's swivelling head.

'Aw, slow down, Snag!'

'Well, why'd ya get them for, anyway? Old Snow sees you walk in with that lot he'll probably have another heart attack?'

'Well, what else was there?'

'Fruit?'

'We don't know if he can eat, Snag.'

'Well, Ike? As you of all people should know, if he can't eat he probably won't want to look at flowers much, either?'

'You ever seen him eat fruit?'

'Certainly never seen him gazing at flowers, Ike?'

'Well shit, Snag — what was I supposed to bring, packet of smokes and some beers?'

'Ah, skip . . .' But then Snag wheels so abruptly into Ike's cannas that the two of them stand for a moment in a paralysed embrace, their faces pressed into opposite sides of the bunch. *'Fucking hell, you see what I see, Ike?'*

Through the flowers, above Snag's head, Ike looks into the casualty waiting-room at the end of the corridor, and there spies a two-headed beacon of flames — red Mohawk hair and yellow golf cap.

Is there a flicker of panicky recognition in the dark man's eyes, as the two of them limp arm in arm past the cannas?

'Call it quits, Jackson.'

'You drown, I O.D., Wallace?'

'Seems fair,' says Wallace with shaky gaiety. 'Only next time you mutiny, sailor-boy, make sure I can breathe water.'

'And, Wallace, you make sure *I* . . .', Jackson's riposte cut short by the door that closes on Wallace's raucous tremolo of laughter, on Jackson's act of snatching his yellow cap-brim round to watch his back as he exits.

'You're not going to believe this, Snow . . .'

The grey face looks up at them, and old Snow's lips shift with the beginnings of a grin — here's that silly fat bugger Ike with a bloody great bunch of . . . and young Snag, all worked up about something, leaning over — *You're not going to believe this, but . . .*

Pulling the grin back into his mouth, he tries to say the words . . . *all you need's a Huntley and Palmer cream cracker . . .*

'. . . but you'll never guess who we saw just now, Snow? When we came . . .'

Ike's big smile nodding away there behind the flaming flowers.

'Remember those people with the flash red car? Always at the . . .'

'Right, Snow, the Porsche,' Ike nodding into his flowers.

'. . . at the — what? Porsche, right — they was, they were just staggering out of . . .'

'Always at the carwash.'

'Jeez — shut up, Ike?' And she turns her head over her shoulder, so impatient, trying to be gentle. And then her little face's looking down at him again, her eyes are running around looking at him, and her spiky hair all bright with the light behind it, and Ike's big bunch of red flowers there, too. Her mouth busy with smiles over words he doesn't really want to listen to, he just wants to flaming look at her.

. . . all at once, one day, it was as though she just caught in the corner of his eye, so vivid and young — he felt old.

But I could be her . . .

But I'm old enough to be her . . .

And it was a relief at first, to find himself thinking she could

150

be his daughter, because it'd felt wrong when she first caught in his eye like that — she was so little — okay for young Ike, fat as he was — but it made *him* feel like a dirty old bugger. Loco — smashed up his kid's bike and biffed stones on the roof!

But I'm old enough to be her father.

It was all right. It wasn't like that.

You're not going to — and just kept grinning at the thought of her, or when he saw her skylarking there at smoko or giving the boss the runaround. What a flaming little holy terror!

And then, as well, like he really hadn't for years, he'd kept remembering the burning sunhats and belting up the little bike with his Kelly hammer, and the worker's hut at Hillcrest camp, Kinleith.

'Snag, I never chucked any stones on the roof, Snag, honest to God . . .'

'What's he saying, Snag?'

'Can't hear, Ike — here, take it easy, Snow? No need to . . .'

'Maybe he can't, Snag?'

'Can't what?'

'Can't . . . talk.'

'Why the hell would she want to tell the kids I done something like that, Snag? That I stood outside the flaming hedge and biffed stones on the roof? And never seen them again, Snag.'

'What was that, Snag?'

'Something about biffing stones, Ike. Jesus. Here, take it easy, Snow? He's crying, Ike!'

'Maybe we better . . .'

But Snag leans down and kisses the grey-stubbled cheek, its trickles, its persistent nicotine smell, its sour breath. Then she sits on the edge of the bed, she puts her face down by Snow's.

'Tell you what, you go, Ike? I'll stay for a bit.'

'What about . . . ?', holding out the huge lilies.

'Give them to the . . .'

'I'll stick 'em in the . . .' Ike rams them into the water carafe. 'See you soon, Snow. Good t' see you looking, good to . . .' His immense backside moves swiftly from sight.

'Good old Ike.'

151

'What was that, Snow?'

But he closes his eyes against the light. He can feel her breath by his cheek. What does it matter now — all that bullshit, flaming years ago, the burning Foreign Legion hats, the smashed bike — glitter of hosewater by the strawberries, red blood down the driver's shirt — the kidlings.

Lifting his hand from the coverlet, he drops its against Snag's head — the fair hair looks spiky, but it's soft, like a kid's, and he can feel the warmth of her skull through it. He feels her hand come up to cover his.

'You're going to be all right, Snow. Tough as old boots, eh?'

And when she feels he's asleep, his breath roaring shallowly in his throat, his hand slipping from her head to the coverlet, she sits up and takes a look. The old turtle mouth hangs open, a rheumy seepage leaks under the eyelids. In the greyish skin, his big purple nose has gone a lavender colour. The nose and the ears seem biggest — outsized, as though all that's left is to breathe and listen.

His chest pants with a kind of limping rhythm — *tramp flop*.

'Listen, Snow,' whispers weeping Snag by the great ear, 'I never told anyone before? When I was twelve, my old man used to come in at night, into my room. He started to smell of sherry. At first, all I got was his breath — Goodnight darlin', he'd say, he'd give me a kiss? Then he used to sit on the bed for a while. After a few weeks he'd get drunker than ever. He used to try to talk to me, Snow? I was twelve. I didn't know what it was about, but I felt sorry for him. Then I started to get scared, because he'd sometimes cry, and then ask me not to tell Mum about it? I used to get scared of him coming in — 'bout twice a week, it was — he'd come in drunk and breathe sherry all over me, and then sit mumbling on the bed — "Y'unnerstan', y'unnerstan'?" — he used to say that. I'd never been scared of him before — he was neat to us kids. But something was going wrong? He just started to change? The more scared I got, the more sorry for him I got too, and the more worried. The more worried I got, the more I couldn't tell Mum about it? There was nothing to tell, anyway. Just . . . worried.'

Snag moves her lips right up by Snow's ear.

'One night . . . I locked my door? I just couldn't stand the thought of him breathing on me, and crying maybe the way he did sometimes. Then I heard him at the door? It was always when Mum was out — she was out two or three times a week, working. I heard the door-handle rattle, Snow? Then I got really scared — it was like I knew it was a mistake to lock the door. It was going to make things go wrong. I mean, it wasn't a mistake, Snow, but I was only . . . Jesus, I was only a kid, Snow — what did *I* know? He rattled the door and said to open up, in a loud voice. I thought the others'd hear — my kid brothers? So I ran and opened it — didn't want any noise. He was pretty drunk. It was like he wanted to be angry? Then he just pushed me back to the bed and put a pillow over my head. You know what I'm talking about, Snow. It went on for a couple of months, two or three, once or twice a week, maybe three times a week. I never told anyone, no one but you, Snow. It's been my secret. Can you keep a secret, Snow? Dad went away, someone said it was to dry out at Hanmer Springs, but he never came back. He could be anywhere, really? That's why I went crook at you, Snow, at you and Ike. I'm sorry, Snow. I didn't really mean you? Isn't it a bastard, the things that can happen? Please be all right, Snow?'

When the charge nurse comes in, she finds the pillow next to Snow's head wet with Snag's tears, and a big pool on the night-table where Ike's canna lilies have overflowed the carafe.

'What's been going on here — water ballet?'

Waking, Snow manages a grin, says, 'It's all bullshit.' But the words come out wrongish — the nurse just growls and gets an aide to shove a bed pan under the old bugger.

Snow grinning. *Bullshit.*

That'll be one to tell them when they come back.

Snag, Ike, you're not going to believe this, but . . .

27

NOW THE DISTANT CORDILLERA HAS SUNK IN DARK, THE SEA
between it and the unspoiled fishing village of Island Bay barely
flickers in the light from a nail-paring moon — steely and tremulous, the armoured scales of water.

Not far off, the chains of swings in the children's playground
whack ringingly against hollow stanchions. Slamming the back
door of his secure place, yanking down the bamboo-slat blinds
on the front windows, Salvation shuts out the sound of steel, the
view of cold light. He announces that night has fallen.

'No one can see us now.' His tinny, missionary voice.

The story of Than Giong, as told by Salvation over plates of
rice and salted eggplant and a bottle of Johnny Walker Red
Label, has driven a wedge of memory through Jackson's brain.

On one side of this divide, his father's face swells above the
black Bible he brandishes. Through the windows of the Lock-
wood Home that's replaced the *fale* of his childhood, Jackson can
see the smirking faces of children. Beyond them, where light
bounces up off the blue lagoon, he can see his uncle's aluminium
Parkercraft buzzing in a straight line across the bay — he can
hear it, too; and he can hear that his father's shouting at him
about *fa'a Samoa*. The proper way to do things. The children
outside scatter when his father roars.

Eating ice-cream gateau off Wallace's 'red car' is on the other
side of the divide, and Jackson trembles with fear at the possi-
bility of this side rejoining the one with his Bible-bashing father
in it — trembles first with fear, and then with laughter.

'Joke, Jackson?' — since the morning's immersion, Wallace has
been quick to react to Jackson's moods.

Jackson downs his whisky. The salty eggplant has left his
mouth slimy, his throat parched, and the morning's awful nausea
rises to meet the drink, and welcomes it to the dark pit of

Jackson's belly where a coil of cold laughter stirs and heaves. Icy dragon-breath in his throat — he allows some to escape in a harmless giggle.

'Jackson?'

'Wallace, I was thinking about my father, Wallace.'

Wallace watches Jackson's unshaded eyes traversing from side to side across some mindscape. She doesn't much like that laugh, either. The boy's primed, all right. Any time now. Meanwhile, the paramilitary lulu's eyes seem to be going around in circles — Salvation's not laughing, though. He's looking hard at Jackson between his circle-and-regroup reconnoitres round the smoky shadows of the room. How much to tell? How much to show?

Eye language, thinks Wallace. Christ. Couldn't we have more *action*, yet?

Salvation finds another bottle of Scotch.

'Why, all at once, your father, Jackson?' she says, just to keep the conversation going a little.

'You know what, Wallace? He always say, you, the son of a *matai*, if you don't do something for your people, you'll go to hell. You know where hell is, Wallace?'

Apia on Sunday, thinks Wallace.

'It's when your people won't talk to you no more, and when you got no kids to talk for you, Wallace. When they throw you out.'

'What were you supposed to do, Jackson?'

'Work in a New Zealand factory assembling Japanese cars and send money back to Samoa to buy votes, Wallace.' Jackson's snake of dark mirth writhes again — he puts a hand to his mouth to stop it escaping.

'Shit, Jackson, you going to be sick?'

'No, Wallace. I feel great. I wanna see this Chaffee. This M24 here. That Mr Salvo here told us about. We going to see it?'

'It is dark,' tins Salvation. 'One slow. No hurry.'

'Whaddaya reckon, Wallace? Now? *Naow*?' — and Jackson, gratified, sees heat rise into Wallace's white face. 'Now, Wallace? Mr Salvo? You wanna show me this tank *naow*?'

'Good God,' marvels Wallace. 'Than Giong awakens. The

mute child. The living heart. You think you can drive this thing, Jackson?'

'I'll teach him,' drones Salvation, swallowing Scotch. He pours into their glasses. 'We face the east!' he toasts. 'Than Giong — to ride the iron horse!' They drink — Jackson giggles horribly. 'And *mring kongvial* — the spirit animal guardian!'

'That's me, sports,' cheers Wallace, flinging the drink down her long throat.

In his mind's eye, Jackson can see himself driving the tank down the divide between his father's black Bible and Wallace's red sinful delta, to where they converge in black smoke and flames. His dragon lashes.

'Wish you wouldn't laugh like that,' says the *mring kongvial*, shoving her red stripe under Jackson's gasping face. 'Gives me the horrors, Jackson, just a shade.'

'It is time to burn the books again,' salutes Salvation, pouring. Rising to make the toast, Wallace and Jackson fall back heavily — the spirit animal guardian's laughter joins the full roar of dragon-breath.

'Good God, Jackson — let me call you Than — what's come over you?'

Jackson lets the dragon coil itself back down into the cold vault of his bowels.

'Wallace, I think we need a little you-know-what — you know? Straighten everybody out a bit. You got any?'

'You mean you want to dance, fella?'

'Wanna get the inside outside.' Turn the dragon loose. Where the black book meets the burning bush. Where it all runs together.

So that, presently, under the clipping of moon, they are blinded by the dark and stand paralysed in the windy clangour of chains from the playground. And when Salvation has herded them into the shed, and then turns on the big lights, they are blinded again — Jackson flings up an arm across his face which is inches from the 75 mm spout of the Mitchell bomber cannon; and Wallace, opening her eyes again very slowly, peeling the eyelids up, sees the chunky dappled full-frontal features of the

M24 Chaffee light tank right there where she's never till now believed she'll see anything like it; and begins at once to dance.

'Two fast,' exults Salvation. He's not laughing because it's funny, again. But Jackson is — his laughter unfolds massively like a new kind of speech — and like something ancient and legendary.

B.J. HITTING TOP NOTES. 'BUT ONE OF THEM JUST, YOU KNOW, married Miss Galaxy or something! It made the front page of the newspaper, Kate.'

'Can I,' Frank's new line in sarcasm, 'say something?'

'What is it, Frank?'

'Neither of you know shit from fuckin' clay. If it's . . .'

'Why don't you belt . . .'

'. . . listen, if it's on the fuckin' front . . .'

'. . . belt up, Frank! If all, you know, you can do's . . .'

'. . . if it's on the front page of the paper, B.J., then it's not about fuckin' sport, jeez!'

'. . . if all you can do's be abusive, Frank . . .'

'Hang on, B.J. — what was that you said, Frank?' Kate rises from her slovenly beanbag.

'I said, if it's on the front page of the newspaper it's not about sport. If you're into sport, Kate, you turn to the sports pages! Who gives a fuck whether an All Black's married a *sheep*, you know? Miss Galaxy, shit! You read the results, in the sports pages! You don't read the, *you know*, B.J., the *cooking*, or . . . !'

Both women are looking at him. 'You know something? I think he's right,' says Kate.

''Course I'm right!'

B.J. bangs the newspaper on the coffee table. 'All right, then, Frank, what's . . .'

'You know what *I* think?' Quiet Kate picks it up.

'. . . hang on, Kate — what's your bright idea, then, Frank? Stick a pipe through a hole in the wall to that, you know, boxer?'

'If you don't want . . .'

'Why don't you two stop . . .' — Kate carefully turning pages.

'. . . don't want any help from me, don't ask for it next time, you stupid . . .'

'. . . stop bickering — know what . . .'

'. . . stupid fuckin' slag!'

'Frank!' After the crack of B.J.'s slap, a silence falls. One side of Frank's face floods quickly with hectic colour. The other goes white. His mouth sets in a queer smile.

'Know something, B.J.?'

'Oh shit, you know, I'm sorry, Frank.'

'Know something? — No you're not,' he says, still grinning. 'Only thing you've ever been fuckin' sorry for's yourself. But you wanna know something?'

'Sorry, Frank. I didn't . . .'

'*Do* you?'

'. . . didn't mean to — what? Do I want to . . . ?'

'Wanna *know* something, B.J.? Like you say all the time? You know, "*you know*"? I don't reckon you're serious. This is all just a joke. It's just junk, B.J., demo, second-hand. I must've been dreaming! You couldn't pull this, ha ha, pull this off if you tried! You wouldn't know . . .'

'Would you mind . . .'

'. . . you wouldn't know one end of a fuckin' athlete from the other!'

'. . . would you two mind?' Kate's quiet voice. 'You seem to forget there's me. And I'm only into it because it's mad — because I'm sick of saying I'm sorry. Because the thought of that self-righteous prick bringing up my daughter gives me the shits. I don't care what happens. I'll do it all right, Frank.'

'Anyone'd think it was, you know, your idea, Kate.'

'I don't have ideas, B.J., not like you do.' Kate's got to the racing pages.

'Sarcasm won't help, Kate.'

'Listen, this is what I think, B.J. If you don't like it, then . . .'

'Then *what*, Kate?'

'Then you might as well take the freezer back, B.J. As sit around here in this dump slinging off at everything.'

Icy. 'Okay, take turns.'

'Take turns what?' leers Frank through his particolour grin. 'Belting each other up?'

159

'I think she means, take turns picking on her.'

'No, I don't mean that, Kate.' B.J.'s icy formality. 'I mean, take turns picking which sport we should hit.'

'So it's all on, is it?' jeers Frank.

'Of course it's all on.'

'Still the fuckin' A-Team, eh B.J.?'

'You know mine — it's, you know, rugby. It's obvious.'

'All right,' smoothing the newspaper on the table, 'if this is the way we're playing it. Cooperative discussion. Frank's right, the sports pages tell you . . . The one that's always there. Racing.'

'Racing, Kate?'

'Horses.'

Frank's white-and-red face is turned away from them, and in profile they can see that the grin is more like a snarl — he's listening to the sounds of merriment from next door. It must be later than any of them have realised, because the boxer's party has begun to roar from opening and closing doors, and they can hear, quite clearly, a guitar and slurred bursts of song, cackles of shrill laughter, and the sound of someone being screechingly sick in the space between the houses.

'You mean horses, owners, trainers, punters, or fuckin' jockeys, Kate?'

'Be serious, Frank — I mean . . .'

'Well, that's too bad! I mean, you had me there. Stud horses. Now that stuff's worth a mint! Stud fuck. I mean, all over the place there must be these jokers hoping to raise a Melbourne Cup winner in the back paddock, or something.' Frank jabs at the newspaper. 'Here he is. Bonecrusher, for the Japan Cup. You ever see Bonecrusher's thing? About three feet long, B.J.' They can see the thought break into Frank's face. 'Like a *eel*.' The thought stays there while Frank goes on shouting. 'But jocks? Who gives a fuck about stud jocks?' Frank's snarl barely shifts, but laughter comes out through it. The laughter comes from his thought. 'Tell you what *I* think. No one'd give a shit about rugby, it'd just be a joke. There's probably enough little rugby bastards around to start half a dozen new clubs and half the little buggers'd be internationals, too, you know lions and

160

little fuckin' roosters and wallabies and stuff. What's one or two
more organised by a couple of loonies. Couple of . . .'

'I *did* mean horses, Frank.'

'. . . couple of — what? Oh, well then . . .' But Frank's still got
his thought — he's hunting in the newspaper.

'*Horses*, Kate? That's not, you know, a political . . .'

'Forget it! Just stop, B.J.! Yours is political rugby, mine's suddenly turned into non-political horses — what's yours, Frank?
Underwater hockey?'

'Listen to that,' says Frank. He turns his grimace back toward
the boxer's party. 'How're you going to make anyone pay attention to you? You never pay attention to them, even when they're
tearing the fuckin' house down!'

'Just tell us your pick, Frank.'

'Nah — you listen, Kate. You know what I'm talking about.
Next door's a sport party and it doesn't even occur to you to try
walking in there and say, I've got a fuckin' All Black sperm bank
at my place whaddaya think of that? If they was pissed enough,
half of them might think it was a joke and the other half might
want to score! I'd like to see it: Oh, hello, my name's, you know,
B.J., I'm from the All Black Sperm Bank, you know!' Still the
snarling grin. But now it's beginning to be triumphant — beginning to become laughter. 'What've most people got to lose? Fuck
all.' He pulls the evening paper off the coffee table and on to the
floor.

Where it opens at the sports section, where Frank's hand has
been folded within, waiting, is a photograph of an immensely tall
black man leaping high to dunk a basketball.

'You must be joking,' says Kate.

But Frank's not looking at her, at the slow spread of an
outraged, delighted smile across her face, her dawning realisation
of his *coup*. He's looking at B.J., and his snarl opens to release,
finally, not laughter like Kate's, but derisive barks of triumph.

'Glamour sport with, *you know*, a lot to lose,' he says in imita-
tion of B.J.'s lecturing voice. 'It's new, clean, and everybody
loves it. They have these special imported guests. They'd *listen*
to you. This guy's worth money. This isn't some footie hick with

a arse like a shed an', an' a tap like a fuckin' drench gun! This isn't junk. This is ya *eel*, B.J., ya eel man. If youse can pull one of them, I'll forget about the crack you give me just now. I'll even fix the fuckin' freezer.'

It could be broad daylight outside with the heavens opening to let down a shaft of glory — illumination descending upon a new tablet of the law standing there as high as the Bank of New Zealand for all to see; or moonlit valley-night with the clanking windmill's tin vanes flicking around by the dark water, and the sound of a woman's voice singing sea shanties; or it could just be the cops turning up at the boxer's party next door. It makes no difference to B.J. — staring at the imperfect likeness of the tall black athlete upon smeary newsprint.

It's the end. It's this or nothing. When at last you're certain, you realise how uncertain you've always been before. You don't even need to go through with it, though you may.

At last you're serious — you *know*.

Afternoon a Day Later

29

'CAN YOU SEE THAT, SNOW?' THE FAT MAN HOLDS A NEWSPAPER against the side of the oxygen tent within which Snow's eyes sometimes open and seem to be looking. 'Reckon he can see that, Snag?'

Snag's chair is pushed close against Ike's.

'Tell ya what, I'll read it to you, Snow. Can you hear me all right in there? Reckon he can hear me, Snag?'

But Snag, clutching Ike's free hand, doesn't answer — she leans forward on her chair watching the old face that sometimes seems to be watching her.

'You're not going to believe this, Snow . . .', Ike's face freezing aghast at his own tactlessness. 'Reckon you've heard a few good yarns in your time, do you Snow? Well, this one'll, these'll . . .', his face struggling to get the expression right, the way his fluting voice is fighting to find the right way to say things. '. . . these'll knock you, I mean, you won't want to miss — ah, shit, Snag, the poor old bugger can't even hear me, can he?'

Ike's face gives up the struggle to cope — turning awkwardly sideways in their chairs, the fat man and the skinny girl clutch at each other. 'I mean, the most fantastic yarns the poor old bugger will ever have — I mean, he was right there, Snag, he saw all those people, the lot of them — you know, it was all going on just right there all the time, right under his nose, like at smoko, Snag! The poor old bugger never knew, now he'll never know what . . . !'

Open on the floor, the evening paper displays a military tank photographed at dawn on the approaches to the city. Inset, is an indistinct trio of characters. They appear to have formed a short conga-line and to be dancing toward a police paddy-wagon.

Elsewhere on the page is a photograph of the black basketball star Denny McHadden. His eyes and mouth are open toward the camera in a disbelieving expression that is an hysterical parody of the one depicted in the previous day's edition, where the seven-foot star had been snapped potting the winning basket in the final second of the tied National League final. Inset, is a photograph of two women and a skinny youth, all of whom seem to be smiling broadly at the photographer. They have their arms around each other's shoulders. It looks like a holiday snapshot.

When he perks up for long enough to look, Snow can see that the kidlings are hugging each other out there. You can see why they might be a bit upset — it must look like curtains, all right. You might think it was a bit of a flaming shame one turned out so fat and the other so skinny, but in the end what does it matter — even them lies about stones chucked on the roof — probably she was scared I'd take the Kelly hammer to her precious flaming Morris Minor next time, not the kid's . . .

Snow seems to grin — the mouth stretches like a baby's in an ambiguous grimace.

He remembers when he took off after smashing up the bike — three weeks holed up in a bach in the Sounds.

Wasn't even there to chuck stones on the flaming roof! Or was that later?

The kids have got their faces up near that plastic tent thing.

It was a bit like this, really — lying in the little porch out there in the boondocks waiting for that flaming weka to come in the open door same as it did every morning.

'What's that, Snag — is he all right?'

'I reckon the old bugger's fucking well laughing, Ike? Look at that! Bet he is — bloody ol' Snow!'

You're not going to believe this, but . . .

'Shit, Snag, doesn't look like laughing to me — reckon I'd better ring the . . . ?'

'Ike, he's laughing, Ike.'

You're not going to believe this, but all you need's a Huntley and Palmer cream cracker.

It was in the Sounds. I was on me own. I was getting that sick of flaming fish — fish for breakfast, fish for dinner, fish for tea. Nothing else but mussels on the point and cress in the creek.

Nothing else but flaming Huntley and Palmers cream crackers, a bloody great tin of them.

Right, thinks I — it's *got* to be a flaming weka. A chicken dinner, see? You're not supposed to. But they was so tame, if you sat still one'd come up and jab your flaming boot with its beak!

I got to flaming watching them! Couldn't help it — it would start me off thinking about chicken dinner. And no grog, either — I can tell you, I was crook for a while. And fish — God! It was like they wanted me to eat them. They reckon the Sounds is all fished out, but every time I dropped a flaming line in there was a couple of nice snapper, a tarakihi, blue cod. At first I thought this was Christmas, I used to cook 'em down by the beach on a fire and the wekas'd come stalking out of the bush the way they do, and clean up the remains — all that booming they do, and running around after each other's bit of fish. It got so they'd all be there to meet me when I come back with the dinghy. Like a flaming school picnic.

Then I started to really miss the grog — used to lie in the porch in the morning when the sun come in there over the ridge — I'd think, Oh no, not flaming fish again! I'd think about the kids — about bashing up the bike. How she told the cops I biffed stones on the roof to frighten them. Or was that later. What does it matter.

There was this one weka started coming in there every morning — it had this bent foot, see? — must've been in a possum trap or something. Didn't run around much with the rest. I never seen it down at the beach.

I'd be lying there with my eyes shut letting the sun come across the porch to the blanket, I'd hear the little bugger on the wood floor — *tramp tramp tramp*. Only it was crooked, eh. Because one foot used to go out the side, it was all bent, the weka'd just gone on walking on the wrong flaming part of it.

So I'd hear it — *tramp flop tramp flop*, like that — here it came, swinging its leg round like a flaming old soldier or something. Right up to the cot where I wuz lying thinking about stones on the flaming roof and how I wouldn't mind getting stuck into the flaming sewing machine with the Kelly hammer — dying for a cold beer and thinking, mussels or fish, what's it gonna be today, Snow?

You're not going to believe this, but that flaming weka used to come right up and poke at me in bed there! Get up, give us a cream cracker! See, that's what I used to do — give it one of them Huntley and Palmer cream crackers — it used to miss out on all the fish down at the beach.

It was like a flaming pet, that bird. But if I moved too fast in the bed, it'd squirt out a black shit and run for its life — *trampflop trampflop trampflop*! Ha ha! So I had to ease meself out of the blanket real slow, to go inside and get its cream cracker. Then it would just stand off a bit and wait. Oh, it knew, all right! Dag of a bloody thing!

But I wuz getting that sick of fish. After a couple of weeks I got over the grog all right — still knew what I was going to do soon's I got back to the Terminus Hotel in Picton, but I could wait till then — didn't lie there dreaming of the sweat on the glass any more — stopped having that last hunt under the flaming bach for where ol' Fuz put the Scotch. You know.

But flaming fish! Cripes!

Some days I'd try not to catch them! I'd stick bits of bony old spotty on for bait — bam! A lovely big gurnard, croaking away there in the boat. Chuck it back — nothing but the best for bloody Snow! Throw back the same bait the gurnard'd sucked into flaming pulp — bam! A beaut little snapper, flashing away there under the water backwards and forwards by the side of the boat — Get off, get off, you little bugger! Don't fuckin' swallow it!

But in she'd come, too well hooked.

Sometimes I'd only manage to eat half. The wekas'd all be stamping around there booming at each other, crowding around like a pack of kids on a picnic. Let them have it! Let them have the whole flaming lot — *I* don't want it! Couldn't eat another mouthful of fish if it was me last meal on earth!

Not ol' Crooked Leg, though — he wouldn't be there. He'd be hoeing around the bach with his beak — he'd have had his cracker that morning. The old soldier.

Chicken dinners.

I started looking at the shape of those birds, you know? Man, they looked fat! Nice and round.

I started to think, it has to be a weka, Snow, or you'll go flaming mad — you'll go round the twist. Your kids'll never see you again. You'll wash up on the beach, Snow. They'll probably think you was pissed an' fell in, but you wasn't — you was just sick to flaming death of fish!

Rightoh.

'Look at him, Snag! I'm gonna ring the bell, Snag! Snag!'

'Don't, Ike? Not yet? When he's finished.'

'*Finished?*'

'You know. Let him get to the end of it? It's okay, Ike.'

' — '

'Ike, it's okay.'

He heard the weka come in. *Tramp flop.* The morning sun was warm on his blanket. When he opened his eyes he could see the rim of clay the mason bees had built around the porch windows — the early sun struck down through the dusty glass past the green filigree of a ponga fern. The distant line of the ridge had a haze of mist steaming off into the blue sky. He watched a cloud like the one in the Paramount titles at the pictures — it sailed across the window pane. The waves were flopping against the jetty down there. Full tide in the middle of the day. No good for fishing.

Tramp flop.

Looking down along the line of his body stretched out on the old army cot, Snow saw the crippled weka approaching along the wooden floor of the porch. The sun was glossy on its feathers. Its leg swung out and it trod down upon the twisted side of its foot. It turned its head, regarding him with alternate eyes whose bright russet was matched by flecks of auburn among the brown feathers.

From beneath the stretcher, Snow stealthily withdrew a bag of crackers. The weka hesitated. It waited to see what was happening.

Snow took out a cracker and let it dangle in his fingers over

169

the side of the cot. His other hand he cautiously freed from the blanket.

Tramp flop. Tramp flop. The weka advanced again. Its gaze was fixed on the Huntley and Palmer cream cracker.

Tramp.

Flop.

Snow held his breath.

More about Penguins

For further information about books available from Penguin please write to the following:

In New Zealand: For a complete list of books available from Penguin in New Zealand write to the Marketing Department, Penguin Books (N.Z.) Ltd, Private Bag, Takapuna, Auckland.

In Australia: For a complete list of books available from Penguin in Australia write to the Marketing Department, Penguin Books Australia Ltd, P.O. Box 257, Ringwood, Victoria 3134.

In Britain: For a complete list of books available from Penguin in Britain write to Dept EP, Penguin Books Ltd, Harmondsworth, Middlesex UB7 0DA.

In the U.S.A.: For a complete list of books available from Penguin in the United States write to Dept DG, Penguin Books, 299 Murray Hill Parkway, East Rutherford, New Jersey 07073.

In Canada: For a complete list of books available from Penguin in Canada write to Penguin Books Canada Ltd, 2801 John Street, Markham, Ontario L3R 1B4.

Also by Ian Wedde in Penguin

SYMMES HOLE

A New Zealand novel that adds a contemporary whiff of paranoia and conspiracy to the rich tradition of Melville and Kerouac.

In the late 1820s, after a life of hardship and adventure, the whaler James Heberley found his true name and final home in Te Awaiti, New Zealand. In the 1980s a young man in Wellington loses his name and the knowledge of where he is, and sets out to find them. Summoning up the ghosts of Herman Melville and the White Whale, he embarks on a journey through Pacific history that ends in a fish and chip shop on the East Cape.

Symmes Hole is part quest and part historical critique, comic and bitter in turns. It explores and celebrates the underside of official history, and breaks important fresh ground in New Zealand fiction.

'A remarkable and even triumphant achievement, a book that is "serious" and "great", traditional and new at the same time, provocative and beautiful and all those things we would like a big new New Zealand novel to be . . . Its greatest successes are long, long passages of such beauty and conviction that I can't easily think of any writer who comes near him.

'*Symmes Hole* is the most provocative and challenging read I have had for some time.'

Patrick Evans, *NZ Listener*

'It is clever, wise, intelligent, funny, interesting, and above all, stimulating.'

Stephen Danby, *Sunday Times*

'A brilliant tour de force, with a richness of language and texture uncommon in the straight historical novel.'

James Bertram, *Dominion*

'*Symmes Hole* is a complex and sophisticated work, drawing together a magnificently eclectic range of material into a shifting, shimmering collage, finding often ominious links between past and present.'

Ronda Cooper, *Wellington City*

'The action is rampant and the tang of the salty ocean skilfully evoked.'

Daily Post, Liverpool

'An attempt to understand how the drift from frontier status (with all possibilities still open) to gentrified colonialism to commercial exploitation shaped their world, how harpoons and whale oil became nuclear weapons in the Antarctic and hamburgers in Courtenay Place, how history and memory continually transforms, continually eludes.'

The Scotsman